Switching It Up

A SAFE Security Novel

Michele Zurlo

www.michelezurloauthor.com

Switching It Up (SAFE Security 2)
Copyright © August 2017 by Michele Zurlo
ISBN: 978-1-942414-29-2

Editor: Nicoline Tiernan
Cover Artist: Anne Kay

Published by Lost Goddess Publishing LLC
www.michelezurloauthor.com

This e-book is a work of fiction. While reference might be made to actual historical events or existing locations, the names, characters, places and incidents are either the product of the author's imagination or are used fictitiously, and any resemblance to actual persons, living or dead, business establishments, events, or locales is entirely coincidental.

Warning: This e-book contains sexually explicit scenes and adult language and may be considered offensive to some readers. It is not meant for underage readers.

———

DISCLAIMER: Education and training are necessary in order to learn safe BDSM practices. Lost Goddess Publishing LLC is not responsible for any loss, harm, injury or death resulting from use of the information contained in any of its titles. This is a work of fiction, and license has been taken with regard to BDSM practices.

Acknowledgements

Thanks to Juliet Braddock for coming up with the title for this one.

As always, thanks to my editor/wife for all your hard work and tireless support.

Lastly, thanks to my beta readers for your time and hard work!

Table of Contents

Blurb:

As Brea settles into her new life as a D/s switch, treasure hunter, and David's fiancée, her old nemesis Grayson Cuyler resurfaces with a deadly deal. Either David must accept a dangerous, unsanctioned mission or Cuyler will make sure Brea pays for her former life as a thief and con artist. Against Brea's wishes, David and his team take on this impossible task.

Left behind, Brea and her sister/partner-in-crime Jessica hatch a plan that will take them to the Central American country of San Tesoro and put them in the clutches of the man from whom David must steal the prize that will save or doom them all.

Warnings: BDSM, sensory play, anal sex, sex toys, D/s role switching, and chocolate frosting

David: In Service to the Sugar Queen

"Sit tight, my precious thief. I'm coming in one minute."

Brea's voice carried through the apartment and into the bedroom where I patiently waited for my fiancée to join me. I'd prefer to call her my submissive, but considering that I was the one bound to the bed with leather cuffs, that would be a reach.

Speaking of reaching, I had an itch on my inner thigh that was driving me crazy. I tried rubbing my thighs together, but that just seemed to increase the radius of the irritation. Since only my wrists were immobilized, I shifted and scooted, trying in vain to get my thigh closer to my hand. I leaned to the side to move my head out of the way and hiked up my leg, but I only succeeded in banging my head.

"David? Are you all right?" She started her query in the kitchen, but she ended it in the doorway to the bedroom. Over a sexy blue silk-and-lace teddy, she wore an apron that read: *Your Opinion isn't in MY Recipe.*

No way in hell I was going to tell her I wasn't. "Peachy."

She motioned to my awkward position, raised leg and all. "Whatcha doing?"

"I have an itch?"

Her emerald eyes lit, and she laughed, a bubbly sound that effervesced from deep inside, but she made no move to come closer. "Where?"

"Inner thigh." Slowly I scooted back into the position she'd left me, and I leveled my best Dom look directly at her. It's firm, the kind that used to have her scurrying to obey, and it clearly ordered her to scratch my itch. She didn't move. "Payback's a bitch."

At this she snorted and rolled her eyes. "Yeah, because you aren't planning payback for this entire evening." She left, probably heading back to the kitchen to finish frosting the dozens of cupcakes she'd made for her brother to take to work.

I really didn't think she'd be back quickly, so I was pleased to see her return immediately. This time, she had a clear glass mixing bowl in one hand, streaks of dark brown frosting interspersed with areas she'd cleared away. If I hadn't been tied down, I would have snagged it and licked the bowl clean. She set it on the bedside table and sat with one knee and half her ass on the edge of the bed.

"You know, Leon doesn't expect you to actually make the cupcakes."

She lifted a spatula full of frosting from the bowl. "I always settle my debts. He won them fair and square after beating me twice."

They'd been arm wrestling, and I didn't think the contest had been fair. Leon was my size, and my little sub wasn't. She was cute and sweet and probably planning to kick my ass for suggesting those were reasons she shouldn't be as strong as Leon or me. "It was rigged."

She shrugged and slid the spatula over my right nipple, coating it with her homemade chocolate frosting. "It was a sibling bonding ritual, something to make up for all the times I didn't kick his ass when we were kids." With her index finger, she scooped the rest of the chocolate from the spatula. Then she held her delightful finger to my lips. "But I don't want to talk about him right now, my precious cupcake thief. I want to do things to your body—sinful, decadent things to punish you for stealing from the Sugar Queen. And since you're tied up, you have no choice but to lay here and take it."

This arrangement hadn't been on my bucket list. When I'd first started in the lifestyle, I'd bottomed for a woman on whom I'd had a huge crush. I hadn't hated it, but the experience was enough for me to understand that I wanted to be in charge.

So how did I come to be in this situation? Simply put, my lovely submissive was a switch—or at least she was experimenting with switching. Since I wasn't going to let her indulge with someone else, I found myself naked and bound to my bed while the woman I loved beyond anything in this world fed me chocolate frosting from her fingertip.

My gaze slid from her green, almond-shaped eyes to the engagement ring she sported on her left hand. The central gem, a large, square-cut diamond, glinted in the lamplight. A nest of emeralds surrounded it. The ring matched her collar, a necklace that featured a jewel-encrusted lock inscribed with both our names. For this scene, I'd removed the collar. She caught the drift of my gaze, and she set her hand on my chest. I wanted so badly to touch her, to cover her hand with mine and entwine my fingers with hers.

She slid her fingertips over my skin, caressing with a feather-light touch, and leaned until her lips were inches from mine. "Remember your safewords?"

"Yep." They were the same as hers. No sense in getting fancy. Plus I didn't intend to use them. I'd put impact and any kind of pain play on my list of hard limits. It wasn't that I didn't trust in her abilities, more that I was loath to give up control. This was as far as I was willing to go, and I only did it because it was what she needed. Even as a bottom, I was still her Dom.

"Still itchy?"

I shook my head.

"Good." A glint of evil gleamed from her eyes. "It's time for you to pay. Cupcake thieves are dealt with quite harshly in these here parts."

Her accent changed from British to Old West by the time she got to the end of her threat. I struggled not to laugh. Instead I pasted on a pouty frown. "You can't prove I took those cupcakes." I may have accidentally eaten half a dozen cupcakes when she wasn't looking, and that may have landed me in this current predicament. It was a hardship to live with a gifted baker and be prohibited from touching the goods.

With a grin, she untied her apron and tossed it onto the chair next to the table. The blue lace caressed her breasts and floated down her midsection, stopping just before her panties began. Her sensual curves stole my breath.

"Damn, Sugar. You are beautiful."

"That's Sugar Queen to you, thief."

No way in hell I was going to call her by that name. Though we were role playing, it was too much like a title, and I had refused to use titles when she topped me. There was only so much control I was willing to give up.

"I'll have your confession soon enough." She bent over and sucked the frosting from my nipple. The moist heat of her mouth lit a fire inside me, and when she scraped her teeth across my nipple, I couldn't suppress a moan. She pressed her nail against the skin over my ribs and scratched a single line down to my knee. Okay, I'll admit that I liked when I drove her wild during sex and she used her talons to score long scratches on my arms and back. Maybe I had a small streak of masochist. Another moan escaped from my depths, and she repeated the move.

My hands itched to touch her, and I jerked on the restraints. Chains rattled against the solid mahogany headboard. "Untie me, and I'll do incredible things to your body, Sugar."

She scratched me once more, but this time she ended up at my inner thigh. Her fingers caressed my sac, and she gave it a gentle squeeze. When I was in charge, I didn't play fairly. I'd used clamps on her clit and labia, and I'd penetrated her with very large dildos. Dreading what she had in mind for my boys, I closed my eyes. She fondled my testicles for a little while, and it felt so good, but then she changed her grip and slowly pulled down, stretching my balls. Expecting pain, I exhaled. To my surprise, it didn't hurt. The strange sensation added fuel to the fire, and I opened my eyes to see her intently watching my reaction.

Devious bits of triumph quirked her delicious lips into a sensual smile. "Who's got your balls?"

I blinked, not knowing what she wanted. "You do."

She pulled harder, elongating my sac to the point of discomfort, but this development curiously didn't impact my growing erection. "Say my name, you naughty, naughty man."

"Sugar, if you pull any harder, you're going to break important equipment."

Instead of pulling more, she twisted them ever so slightly. A pleasure-pain combination shot down my legs and up my spine, and I exhaled hard. "Sugar Queen. Say it."

I gave in. She owned my heart and soul already. I'd already given her everything that mattered, and now she held my future in her hand. "Sugar Queen."

She eased the pressure, slowly releasing her hold. "There now. Was that so hard?" Without waiting for my response, she crossed to the armoire and opened the doors on the top half. She selected several implements and brought the armload back to the bed.

I identified two more leather cuffs and a spreader bar, but the other items she'd brought were small, and wrinkles in the bedcover hid them from my view. She buckled a cuff around each of my ankles, and then she attached the spreader bar to one of them. I wasn't sure how I felt about that, but as I mentally ran down the vast list of limits I'd set, I realized a spreader bar wasn't on there. So when she scooted my legs apart, I cooperated.

Next she smeared chocolate frosting over both my nipples and my lips. I licked my lips because Brea's homemade frosting was damned tasty. She grinned, so I figured she wasn't upset by that move, but her impish giggle had me rethinking whether that had been a good idea. Brea was a bratty sub, and I had the sinking feeling that Brea as a Domina was a brat without limits.

She returned the spatula to the bowl, and then she reached for something by my feet. The scrap of fabric hadn't been on my radar, but I recognized my favorite blindfold. Scratch that—it was only my favorite when I was using it on her. She slipped it over my eyes and tightened it down. Then she felt around the edges, adjusting it to let in no light.

Deprived of my favorite sense, I mentally sharpened the others. This was no different from tracking down a target in the dead of night without benefit of night vision goggles. The scent of chocolate frosting grew stronger, and the cuffs imprisoning my wrists and ankles grew tighter and heavier. The featherlight caress of Sugar's hands moving over my skin became the focal point of my experience.

Forcing myself to relax, I gave myself over to her ministrations. My sub wanted to tie me up and touch me. I reaped the reward for letting her be in control this one time. Just as I was coming to terms with this change in dynamic, she chuckled. The low sound was full of naughty delight. I tensed as she took my dick in hand.

I wasn't hard, though I was definitely heading in that direction until something cold and hard replaced the warm, soft caress of her fingers. She pushed it down to the base of my cock, and then I felt something brush against the crown of my cock.

"Sugar? What the hell are you doing?"

A loud, sharp slap stung my inner thigh. "You'll address me as Sugar Queen, or you will be punished even more, my precious thief."

I needed to get control of this situation. "Yellow."

She didn't let go of my cock, but she did pause with whatever she was doing to it. "What's wrong?"

"Is that a cock ring? We didn't talk about cock rings."

"Yes, it is a cock ring. What freaks you out about a cock ring?"

Besides the fact that I'd never used one and wasn't looking forward to orgasm denial? While I loved denying Brea—or not giving her permission to climax while forcing her to have one—I didn't want to be on the receiving end. "Don't they hurt?"

"Only if you try to take it off while you have a hard-on. Trust me. I would never do anything to damage Little Sir. He brings so much joy into my life."

I'd given up on asking her to stop calling my dick by that name. With an ungracious sigh, I said, "What else are you putting on me?"

"David." She infused my name with a sharp reprimand. "You're not in control right now. I know this is hard for you, but you can't call yellow just because you're not in charge."

"You're supposed to be nurturing and reassuring right now." I frowned to emphasize the sour grapes I was feeling.

She released my cock, and the bed dipped on either side of my ribs as she straddled my torso. Then she eased the blindfold off and nailed me in the eyes with a steady gaze. "If you needed coddling right now, I'd give that to you. But you're mostly trying to be in control even though you're the one tied to the bed. I trust you to honor my limits, and you have to trust me to do the same." She caressed my cheek. "I'm not new to being a Domina."

6

I studied her for the longest time, not because I doubted her but because I was waging an internal war. She needed this. To my core, I knew she needed this, and I dug deep for the strength to give it to her. This time when I exhaled, I released all my tension. "All right, Sugar Queen. Green."

She slid the blindfold back in place, and then she kissed me. Her tongue slid along my lower lip before slipping into my mouth. She controlled the kiss, but I kissed her back with all the passion I had. Then she kissed a path along my jaw and nipped at my earlobe. "Thieves who behave and repent, who serve their queen well, are rewarded."

Shifting again, she climbed off me and resumed whatever she was doing to my cock. The light touches and strokes roused it to stand at attention. So far, the cock ring wasn't a factor. When the heat of her mouth closed around my hard-on, I forgot all about the ring. Brea gave great head. With a moan, I lifted my hips to thrust into her sweet mouth. I tried to bring my hand down to encourage her, but the restraint did its job.

Before long, she stopped, leaving my dick throbbing with unsated desire. I wanted to protest, but another sensation had me gasping. Pinpricks, just sharp enough to register, crawled up my thigh, over my stomach, and along the undersides of my arms. Back and forth, up and down, the sensation moved. I'd run a pinwheel over my flesh before, but it hadn't felt like this at all. I don't recall being impressed one way or the other, and so I'd never used it on a sub.

But there was something about being bound and blind that intensified the small pricks and turned them into something titillating. By the time she made a second circuit, my body trembled with uncontrolled pleasure, and I moaned loudly.

She kissed me again, nipping at my lower lip as I tried to capture hers for a deeper kiss. With that evil chuckle that was growing on me, she trailed kisses lower, peppering my neck and shoulders with soft kisses and stinging bites. I didn't remember until her mouth closed around my nipple that she'd frosted me there—and it occurred to me that she'd probably frosted my dick before she'd sucked it. My Sugar Queen.

By the time she straddled me and sank down on my cock, I was more than ready. Silk grazed my skin as she slid the blindfold off, and my gaze went immediately to the point where our bodies were joined. She'd removed her panties, but she'd kept the top of the teddy on, and the lacy blue silk brushed against my stomach as she leaned forward.

With one finger, she worked her clit, and her other hand cupped her breast. Through the fabric, she rolled her nipple. I loved to watch her come, and the show she put on made me hotter. I wasn't sure how much longer I was going to last. Her body arched and writhed, and she lost her rhythm as she came with a loud shout. I relaxed to let my climax come, but it didn't.

Brea stopped, her chest rosy and heaving with evidence of her orgasm. Without ceremony, she climbed off me. My cock slid out of her slick pussy and fell to the side, its purpled head pulsing with need. The rest of my body trembled with a lust that was driving me out of my mind.

She flopped onto her back, sending a tiny shockwave through the mattress. "That was magnificent, my precious cupcake thief."

"It would have been better if you'd waited for me."

A weak laugh shook her chest. The top of her teddy had slipped down, so that's where I was looking. "I'm not finished with you, hot stuff. You were very naughty, and you must learn your lesson."

I knew she'd been a ball-buster of a Domina, but that didn't stop me from shooting off my mouth. "The moment you untie me, I'm going to touch you all over. I'm going to kiss you breathless and fuck you until you can't walk anymore."

This time her laugh came stronger. She rose up on her knees and bent over me, the soft silk brushing my stomach as she peered deep into my eyes and locked onto my soul. "I love a prisoner who thinks he can misbehave and get away with it. Don't make the mistake of thinking I can't keep you in line, my precious."

She kissed me, a string of stinging bites on my lips, neck, and jaw. I arched and groaned, jerking hard on the restraints in hopes of splintering the bed posts to free my arms. Unfortunately I'd purchased the bed frame with bondage in mind. The thing was solid and sturdy.

Her palm skated over the crown of my cock, and an electric jolt went through me. I growled. With a delighted giggle, she captured my mouth in a lingering kiss. The moment her tongue teased between my lips, I relaxed and let her have control. This wasn't submission on my part—it was strategy. Okay, after a few seconds, there might have been a little bit of surrender. She was a damn fine kisser. Her lips were the perfect combination of soft and firm, and she knew how to do magical things with her tongue. I lost myself in the spell she wove.

It took a little time for me to realize my arms were free. The slight weight of the leather cuffs still encircled my wrists, but she'd released the carabiner clip binding the cuffs to the eyehooks on the headboard.

With a victory grunt, I flipped her over. My hands, starved for the feel of her soft skin, roamed her body, seeking but not finding a stopping point. I ravaged her lips, and then I abandoned her mouth to place savage, sucking kisses down her neck and throat. Palming her breast roughly, I squeezed the handful before rolling her nipple through the silky lingerie.

Through it all, she hadn't acquiesced by any means. She kissed me back as fervently as I kissed her, and she raked her nails across my shoulders and down my back. I felt her fingernails dig into my ass before her hand slid around to slip between us. I lifted, giving her permission to guide my cock into her welcoming warmth.

The wildness had gone out of her, and by the time she gently gripped my balls, I realized the genius of her countermove.

Lifting my mouth from her collarbone, I gazed into her clear, green orbs. "If you break those, you'll never get to have kids."

Her husky laugh filled the space. "You seem to have forgotten who is in charge, my precious cupcake thief. You're going to stand at the foot of the bed, where I'm going to secure your bindings. We're going to move slowly because I'm not going to let go of you."

To emphasize how serious she was, she slowly pulled down on my boys. A strange pleasure-pain combination curled my toes and had me involuntarily arching my back. Was I trying to get closer or farther away? I honestly couldn't say.

With my manhood at stake, I cooperated as she maneuvered me to stand at the foot of the bed. This was not easy with her holding onto my boys and the spreader bar still attached to my ankle cuffs. Our bed had four sturdy posts, though the footboard didn't reach the top of the mattress. I moved an inch at a time.

"Secure the binding on your left hand." The hold she had on my balls tightened, and it felt half like she twisted them and half like she was massaging them. It didn't hurt, but the sensation was equally thrilling and puzzling. I'd never pictured myself as the cock-and-ball-torture type.

I attached the carabiner to the eyehook. She kept one hand around my balls and snapped the carabiner on my right wrist cuff to the other eyehook. It latched into place with a soft click that sealed my fate. With one last, light squeeze, she released her stranglehold on my balls.

The whole time she studied my face. Her intent expression had me wondering what I looked like when our positions were reversed. Did the way I looked at her make her feel like she was the center of my universe? I hoped so, because the way she was looking at me made me feel cherished and important.

A triumphant smile transformed her face from beautiful to breathtaking, and I could only stare in awe at the woman who had become my reason for living.

She pressed a quick kiss to my cheek, and then she disappeared from view.

"Sugar?"

A sharp smack to my ass caught me by surprise.

Rather than chastise her for engaging in impact play against my wishes, I accepted the light punishment—it hadn't hurt—as the correction she'd intended. I cleared my throat. "Sugar Queen?"

"What is it, my precious?"

"I'm a much better lover when I can use my hands."

By way of response, she buckled cuffs above my knees and attached them to the bedposts. Though she removed the leather restraints from my ankles, which meant the spreader bar was now gone, my stance was wider—and I was more vulnerable.

I felt her fingertip on my anus, smearing lubricant across the tight muscle there. Anal play hadn't been on my list of limits—hard or soft— and right about now I was seriously considering calling yellow. I held off for now, reasoning that she'd trusted me in this regard, and so I needed to afford her the same latitude. My cock began to soften.

"I hadn't planned to do this today, my precious, but you misbehaved, and naughty thieves beg to be brought in line. Relax. This won't hurt. I'm going to count three, and then I want you to exhale."

She counted to three, and I exhaled. I felt a small sensation, neither pleasure nor pain, and then nothing. Had she changed her mind?

As I analyzed the lack, she came around and climbed onto the bed. Kneeling in the center, wearing only the top of the lacy blue teddy and gazing at me with undisguised lust, she was utterly sexy. I jerked on the restraints, but my action only brought a bratty curve to her sensuous lips.

She lifted the edges of the lingerie and tugged it over her head, baring the full force of her luscious curves. Then she sucked on her fingertip the same way she had sucked on mine so many times before, her lips forming a perfect bow. After a few seconds, she slid that finger down her body to circle her clit. My dick, which had been heading toward resting position, hardened instantly. She ran her hands over her hips and thighs, across her stomach, and she cupped her breasts. She touched herself in all the ways I yearned.

I pulled harder, fighting the restraints, and she settled onto her back. I hadn't noticed the vibrator tangled in the bedcovers, but I knew exactly which one it was the moment she picked it up. It wasn't very large, but it was powerful. I'd tortured her to orgasm with it just the other evening. She slid it through her juices and turned it on the lowest setting. I watched her play, seconds stretching into hours. Normally I loved watching her masturbate—I often required her to do so—but when I was in control, everything was different. I loved watching her body move, shades of passion dance across her lovely features, and though this was the same, it was completely frustrating to not be able to touch her.

She turned up the speed on the vibrator and slid it into her dripping pussy, and her gaze locked onto mine. Frustration and desperation morphed into acceptance, and urgency simmered just below the surface. Her moans grew louder as she neared climax, and my cock throbbed as she went over.

Moments passed, and she withdrew the toy from her body. She came to me on her knees, again not the same as when she was my sub, and unfastened the clips holding me in place.

She smiled softly, an expression that managed to be both sated and hungry. "You've been very good, my precious thief. Now you may fuck me until you come."

I didn't need to be told twice. I leaped on her, wrestling her to the mattress even though she went willingly. Wrapping my fist in her hair, I pulled her head back and licked the long column of her throat. I kissed her flesh as I nudged her legs farther apart, and then I sank into her hot pussy. Those swollen tissues welcomed me. They pulsed and caressed, sucking me deeper. I held her to me, gripping her shoulders, her head, or handfuls of her ass as I pumped every ounce of pent-up passion into her body.

Incoherent but sexy noises purred in her throat and poured from between her lips. She gazed at me, eyelids half closed, as she writhed in my arms. Her hands never stopped moving. She caressed my face, squeezed the back of my neck, raked her nails over my flesh, gripped my shoulders, back, or ass—and her movements grew wilder as she lost herself in bliss.

She came once, twice—and still I couldn't seem to climax. Her pussy pulsed around my cock, urging it toward that peak. Suddenly my vision went white. I fell from the edge of a cliff I hadn't known was there. My balls drew up, and my orgasm detonated, shattering my spine with a pain that enhanced the bliss. My shout became a whimper because my vocal chords were paralyzed. I collapsed, crushing Brea because I didn't have the strength to shift my weight to the side.

I drifted on soft currents of air, insane pleasure washing through my system with the regularity of my heartbeat. Sometime later, I became aware of Brea pressing a cool cloth to my brow. I was on my back, and her naked body was stretched out beside mine. Her boob rested against my arm. I wanted to touch it, but I either lacked sufficient will or energy to move.

"Sugar?"

"I'm here." She lifted the warmed cloth, waved it in the air, and then she put it back on my forehead.

I appreciated the coolness. "That was amazing."

"I'm glad you thought so."

"Am I slurring my speech?"

"Yes. You don't have to talk right now. Let me take care of you." She sat up and massaged my arm from shoulder to wrist.

It wasn't really sore, but her touch felt good, and I would never turn down a massage. I glanced down, and that's when I noticed the cock ring was gone. "Did it come off okay?" Metal rings could be problematic if left on for too long or if they were too small.

Her giggle had a hint of devilry. "Yes. I had it made special for you. I even had it inscribed like the ring in The Lord of the Rings movies. I took the butt plug out before I turned you over."

"Thanks." The less said about that, the better. "Can I see the ring?"

"Not unless you're ready to wear it again." She climbed over me and massaged my other arm.

I lifted the cloth away from my face and nailed her with a hard frown. "Sugar."

"Nope. I'm not bending on this issue. That's mine, for use when I'm in charge. If you want one for when you're in charge, I can give you the measurements I used. They worked really well."

My frown turned doubtful. "When did you measure my dick?"

She snorted. "I'm good with dimensions, and I'm very familiar with it, so I didn't need to measure. I estimated."

I couldn't argue her point, and the ring had worked just fine. "Why didn't you go with leather for the first time?"

"I know what I'm doing." She finished massaging and snuggled against my side. Her head rested on my shoulder, and I pulled her even closer.

There was no arguing her point, so I changed the subject. "Have I told you yet today that I love you?"

She tilted her face up to look at me, a wealth of love shining from her green eyes. "Yes, but you can say it again."

I brushed light kisses across her eyelids and cheeks. "I love you, Sugar."

"I love you too." Her lips met mine for a tender follow-up.

Brea: Flea Markets and Other Pests

"I could clean this up, put a glass top on it, and I bet we could get three or four hundred for it." Jessica knelt on one knee next to a metal trough. It was about three feet long and eighteen inches wide. Rust mottled the surface.

Crouching down next to her, I ran my hand over the surface to see how much had disintegrated into rust. "You're serious about making upcycling part of our store?"

She shrugged. "We have a storefront. Might as well put my artistic eye to use. You're great with the mechanical aspects. Together we could have a cute little shop."

When Dean had gifted us with retail space on the first floor of the SAFE Security building, we'd used it to open a small museum to display the treasure we'd discovered at Murder Rocks a few months before. While we had a fairly steady stream of patrons interested in a free look at some Missouri history, we also had a lot of would-be customers who wanted to purchase artifacts. We had yet to sell anything, though, because Jessica and I couldn't agree on what we wanted to keep and what we wanted to sell.

For display cabinets, we'd been refinishing and repurposing garage sale finds. People had asked about purchasing some of those items as well. Last week Jessica had sold a table she'd upgraded—she'd glued an old window frame to an end table with a warped surface and topped it with clear plexiglass—for almost ten times the cost of materials, she had talked nonstop about trying it again.

I wasn't against it, but I didn't want to spend all my time building and refinishing furniture. It had been months since I'd cracked a safe, and I hadn't been invited to go on any adventures with David and his friends. To be totally honest, I missed sneaking around and breaking into places. However, since the last time, when my actions had rained catastrophe on everyone I loved, I'd been good. I'd been very, very good, and I was finding that it didn't bring the same kind of satisfaction as being bad.

Jessica put her hand on my arm. "What's wrong?"

I shrugged. "Nothing. You're going to need a frame to make a stand for this thing. You can't just set it on the ground."

"It'd be too low," she agreed. "I'm thinking wood. We could stain it dark and paint the trough an eggshell white. The contrast will be eye-catching. I could stage it with some fake flowers inside, so people could see the ways they can change it up to go with their décor."

We stood and studied it. I was sure she was thinking of exactly how it would look once she was finished with it, but I was thinking about the man standing three stalls over. He'd been sticking close to us since we'd arrived at the flea market a little over an hour ago.

Jessica took my hand. "Little sister, I know when something isn't right with you."

Yes, she did. And unlike other people, I found Jessica impossible to manipulate into changing the subject. "I want to find another treasure. I could do without the kidnapping this time, but wouldn't it be cool to find something else to add to our collection? And I'm thinking we should name our shop."

Right now, the temporary sign on the door simply read Treasure Museum. If we were going to sell unique furniture—and if we ever agreed on which pieces of treasure with which to part—then we'd need to incorporate the business. Currently we were operating under the umbrella of SAFE Security.

"Zinn's Treasures."

Though I now claimed Zinn as my surname, I didn't feel any special connection to it. "B and J's Furniture Shop and Treasure Museum."

Jessica shot me a long look. "B and J? We have unfortunate initials. How about Jessica and Brea's Furniture Shop and Treasure Museum?"

"That's a really long name."

"We could put our names in larger size, and then use the rest as a subtitle." She squeezed my hand. "You have ideas for which treasure we could go after next? And will loverboy let you do it?"

David and I had discussed the idea of me going after lost treasure in vague terms. We both assumed I'd do it, but since I wasn't actively in pursuit of anything, he treated it like a dead issue. "He doesn't have veto power. He might voice objections, but he can't stop me."

"I kind of want to call it Murder Rocks, with the furniture and treasure parts as a subtitle." Jessica wrapped her arm around mine and leaned her head on my shoulder. "Have you noticed the guy following us?"

"The one three stalls to our right? Yes." In situations like this, we always acted casual. Worst case scenario, they tried to kidnap us. Since we'd been kidnapped at least twice before, that idea no longer frightened us.

"No, the one two stalls to our left. I think there's one the next aisle over, but I keep losing sight of him. He's dressed like the others—khaki dress slacks and a button down shirt. They're going for the young professional look, which won't help them if they're planning to haggle." She pointed out a pair of wooden chairs. The seats looked like they used to be made from woven rattan, but now they were just round holes. "I'm thinking planters. Ivy or some other kind of vine would love the spindles on the backs. Since we're in the city, lots of people would go for something easy and stylish."

I envisioned what she described. "Are you thinking art deco meets bohemian?"

She frowned, and arms still entwined, we wandered closer to the chairs. I set my hand on the top rim and gave it a shake. Two spindles popped out of their holes. The thing wasn't too sturdy. "It's not going to hold a big pot full of dirt."

The owner of the stall came over, a big smile breaking a gap between his shaggy gray beard and overgrown mustache. A chain dangled from the pocket of his well-worn jeans, and his flannel shirt was unbuttoned in deference to the heat of the afternoon sun in March, revealing his Harley Davison T-shirt. The shrewd look in his pale blue eyes hinted at a serious flea market seller. This man likely had the same stall every week during the selling season. "Good afternoon, ladies. I see you're eyeing this great pair of chairs. If you put a board across the top of both, you could use it as a bench."

Jessica considered this while I watched out for the three men trailing us. The one to our right chatted with the proprietor of his stall without looking directly at her, while the one to our left wandered to the stall across the path, his attention shifting from us to David and Jesse. The pair stood in the middle of the wide path, absorbed in conversation with each other. I wasn't sure what they were talking about—it was equally likely they were discussing the Royals' last preseason game as it was they were talking about their next case—but since they didn't seem to want company, Jessica and I had gone ahead and left them to catch up.

I untangled my arm from Jessica's, and left her to flirt with the owner of the stall. As I pretended to check out a disassembled bed frame, I caught sight of the man one aisle over. I also counted a fourth man in the stall behind the one where we were.

"Thirty for the pair, and ten for the trough." Since the price tag on the chairs was a hundred and he was asking thirty for the trough, Jessica started low. It was nearing the end of the day, and people were starting to think about all the things they had to load back into their trucks. Late afternoon was the best time for haggling.

The proprietor scratched his beard. "Sixty for the chairs. Twenty-five for the trough."

He didn't come down enough. Jessica shook her head. "Sorry. That doesn't work for me. Fifty for everything. Final offer. It's all I have."

The man grinned and offered his hand. "Miss, you have a deal."

Jessica rooted around in her bag, and she came out with exact change. "It's a pleasure doing business with you, sir."

I picked up the chairs, Jessica snagged the trough, and we trudged back to the guys.

Jesse took the trough from Jessica. Sun glinted from the ends of his very short, light brown hair, and a frown marred his forehead. Dark, reflective sunglasses hid his eyes, but there was no mistaking the censure in his tone. "You shouldn't be carrying things."

Jessica scoffed. "It's light. I'm fine."

Nine months ago, Jessica had awoken from a three-year-long coma. She'd made tons of progress since then, like learning to walk on her own, but she still lacked some of the fine motor skills she'd had before, and she tired easily.

David nodded at the chairs and held out a hand. "Can I help you with those?"

"No, thanks. I'd rather they didn't get broken."

He frowned and stepped closer, his hand coming to rest over mine on the back of one of the chairs. "They're already broken. The seat is missing. Please tell me you're not putting these in our apartment."

I rolled my eyes. "Don't worry. I know how addicted you are to your manly décor—heavy woods, dark metals, and white walls. I'd never do anything to make it look like a woman lives there."

His frown deepened. Twin lines wrinkled between his dark blond brows, and a pit appeared on his chin. "Are we fighting right now? Because I distinctly remember telling you that you were welcome to redecorate."

I couldn't see the chair planter working in our apartment. We didn't have a balcony, and it really wasn't my taste. Still I squared up to him. Now that I was in hissing distance, I threw my shoulders back and stared him down even though I had to tilt my head back to look up at him. "Four men have been tailing us since we got here. Tan khaki slacks and white, button-down shirts."

With his most menacing scowl, he leaned down, stopping with his face inches from mine. "I know, Sugar, and there are actually six of them. Jesse and I have been trying to figure out if they're following you or us."

Without losing my attitude, I said, "And?"

He wrapped one arm around my waist. "And we can't tell." He jerked me to him and pressed a firm kiss to my lips. "Damn, but you're a beautiful brat." Cocky grin firmly in place, he released me.

Jessica rolled her eyes at our public display of affection. "Oh my God, Brea—there's a steamer trunk." She grabbed my arm and ran off.

I raced after her so that she didn't pull my shoulder wrong—she'd grabbed my left arm, which was attached to my bad shoulder. I didn't see what was so fantastic about a steamer trunk, but I figured she was trying to help David and Jesse figure out who the skulking guys were after. Her logic made perfect sense to me. If we split up and they followed us, then the khaki guys were after us. If not, then they wanted David and/or Jesse.

Only David and Jesse weren't on board with that plan. They followed us. Jessica crouched down in front of the trunk and dragged me with her. She ran her hands over the lid and traced the metal decorations on the corners.

"Holy shit, Brea. Do you remember we had one exactly like this in that little walk-up apartment in New Jersey? Someone decoupaged the crap out of this one, but it's otherwise exactly the same."

We may have had a steamer trunk or two in our past, but they'd always been something we'd left behind. Not one of them had sentimental value. But we'd been raised as cons, and so I knew to go with it. "Yes. It was full of books and it had a tea set. We used to set up all our dolls and have a tea party every day at four."

She giggled. "High tea, we called it. You used to put the silver blanket with the embroidered flowers over the trunk to make a table, and I'd heat the water and make little sandwiches."

David and Jesse were behind us. They'd brought along the trough and the chairs. David set the chairs next to Jessica, and Jesse put the trough across the seats. They flanked us, each facing a different direction to keep watch on our followers.

Jesse rested his hands loosely on his waist, and his low voice traveled directly to us. "Run off like that again, and I'll spank the both of you."

I had a hard time swallowing a witty retort, but Jessica couldn't let that go. She lifted a brow at Jesse, a clear challenge. "Is that a threat or a promise?"

He glanced over and lifted his sunglasses. His pale blue eyes were steely and serious. "You won't enjoy it."

Pretending to pout, she stood up and crossed her arms. "That's what you think."

The last time I saw Jessica seriously flirt had been when she was picking up a mark. Actually the only time I ever saw Jessica flirt was for purposes of manipulation. I slowly got to my feet and looked for her to try to pick Jesse's pocket. As evidenced by the fact that the left side of his jacket sagged toward the zipper, his wallet was in the inside pocket.

She gripped the open edges of his jacket and straightened it as she giggled. Under these circumstances, I might expect her to act a little while she took stock of the situation, but from our position, we had a prime view of two of the guys tailing us, and I was reasonably sure I'd picked up a female as well. David and Jesse were in position to see the others. Our formation was perfect, if impromptu.

The fact that she was flirting with Jesse—a man who'd become one of my few friends—set off alarm bells, different ones from those clanging about our situation. I looked at David to see if he was aware of the unexpected flirtation, but he was busy pinpointing the location of our stalkers.

I put my hand on his arm. "Still six, Sir? Including the woman in the aisle behind us?" Using his title signaled that I was prepared to follow his lead.

"Yep. We should head back to Jesse's truck. It's getting late."

"Will the rest of our friends meet us there?" I knew he wanted to draw out the Khaki Brigade, but I wanted to know if Dean and Frankie, the balance of the SAFE Security crew, would be joining us. While I was confident that Jesse and David could take on six attackers, the odds were even better with four against six.

"Not in time."

"Maybe we should shop a little longer." I looked over at Jessica to see that she was still smiling up at Jesse and touching his shirt as she talked to him too quietly for me to hear. "I hope she doesn't pick his pocket."

"He's aware of her habits."

So far she'd only picked someone's pocket when she'd had a little too much to drink (twice—but the first time had saved our lives, so that wasn't a deterrent) and when people were rude to her in public (three times—that I knew about.) I'd confided my concerns about this habit to David, and he agreed to help keep an eye on her. I did not take him to task for telling Jesse because if people we loved were going to be around her, they should have fair warning. I wondered if she considered Jesse's threat as an open invitation for retaliation?

He slung his arm around me and led me back to the chairs and trough. "Jess and Jess, let's get this stuff loaded into the truck."

Both Jesse and Jessica nailed him with a virulent glare. Jessica flounced closer. She hated when people shortened her name, and this was not news to David. Giving him the devil's eye, she picked up the trough, which I took from her. "Payback, David. It's coming for you."

Jesse and David each grabbed a chair. They positioned themselves on the outside of our foursome and herded us toward the parking lot.

"I want the two of you to get into the truck and drive away." Jesse took Jessica's hand, passing his key to her.

Jessica slipped it into her pocket. "We're not leaving you like this. Brea and I have been in our share of fights."

Jesse's chuckle revealed his doubt. "This isn't the same thing."

Our street fights hadn't been as deadly as their mercenary fights tended to be. Nobody had died as a result of their injuries. Those had tended to be turf wars—when you moved as much as we did, sometimes you ended up infringing on someone's territory—and they were over quickly. Sometimes we won, but mostly we lost. I didn't feel the need to point that out to my sister. Besides, Frankie had been teaching me to fight for the past six months.

I put her lessons to use and surveyed my options. "We can't run them over because the parking lot is jammed full of people. There's no room to gather much speed to make a collision worthwhile. Besides, we'd most likely hit one of you two, and I am not in the mood to spend the next several months nursing you back to health."

David laughed. "You're saying you used up your quota of nurturing for the year?"

Since he'd broken his ribs rescuing me from certain death, I'd spent almost two months pampering David. Then I'd spent the last four trying to break him of his dependency. I was not as amused as he was. "Maybe for a couple of years."

"Is there a plan?" Jessica interrupted. "Or are we just willingly heading into an ambush?"

The six members of the Khaki Coalition were now openly following us. They knew they'd been spotted, and they were willing to head to a less populated area to do us in.

"It's not an ambush if you know about it." David's jaw clenched, and I knew he didn't love the situation. "And I'm not going to get my ass kicked by a bunch of idiots in casual office attire."

"We have a plan," Jesse assured us.

"Good to know." Sarcasm dripped from Jessica's voice, the subtext indicating that we didn't know the plan, and she did not appreciate being put in this situation.

The second Jesse's truck came into view, a big black number with an extended cab parked on the grass at the end of a long line of vehicles, I realized that this whole thing might not be about David or Jesse. Grayson Cuyler leaned casually against Jesse's tailgate. He turned as he saw us approach, and he rested his elbow on the truck. Unlike the Khaki Brigade, his jeans and flannel shirt combination blended in with the other flea market shoppers.

Waves of fury washed over me. After his arrest for kidnapping Jessica and me, Cuyler had somehow disappeared from the system, something Brick Dixon, the head of an organized crime ring, had been unable to do. We came to a stop three feet from the bastard.

Before I could consciously process my intention, I dropped the trough, took the chair from David's hands, lifted it back over my shoulder, and swung at Cuyler with all my strength. Cuyler lifted his arm to catch the brunt of the blow. The chair, already rickety, came apart. Sticks of wood burst in all directions, clattered against the truck and bumper, and fell to the grass around Cuyler's feet.

"Hello, sweet thing. I see you missed me."

I cocked my arm back and let loose with a terrific yell, just like Frankie taught me so that I'd hit harder. But my fist never connected with Cuyler's face. David wrapped his arms around me, pinning mine to my sides.

I glanced over at Jessica to see her with her hand parked on her hips, scowling at Cuyler. She shook her finger at him. "You have a lot of nerve."

"I know." He held up a hand. "Believe it or not, I come in peace."

Grunting because I knew I couldn't wrest free from David's hold, I lifted my feet and kicked. "And you'll leave in pieces."

Cuyler danced out of the way, but not before I got a little piece of him. "Simmer down, Autumn. Sorry—Brea. It's going to take some time for me to get used to the name change."

I wanted to say that he'd have plenty of time to get used to it in prison, but he obviously wasn't going to end up in the big house.

Jesse's scowl matched mine. "What do you want?"

"To talk." Cuyler's gray eyes crinkled at the edges when he smiled. He spread his hands to indicate a truce.

It was hard to call a truce when only one side wanted peace. I wanted to break his bones. Memories of the sound of that satisfying crunch would lull me to sleep every night. I stopped struggling against David, and he relaxed his hold.

Cuyler pointed to me. "Are you going to behave?"

"I'll be as good as gold."

David's exhalation meant he'd caught on to my evasion. How good was gold? It had a history of causing problems and hardships. People died over it, and so if I killed Grayson Cuyler, I could say I'd kept my word. He was just another tragic victim of gold fever.

Shoving me behind him—because apparently I was safer near the mercenaries in khaki pants than near Cuyler—David confronted the man to whom I meant to cause great bodily harm. Muscles tightly coiled like a panther ready to pounce, he lifted his chin. "Start talking."

Grayson Cuyler smiled, and though he had a dimple in his right cheek, I wasn't fooled or charmed. "We want to hire you."

David and Jesse exchanged a glance.

Before they could turn him down, Cuyler plowed ahead. "Look, I know you're upset about the Brick Dixon thing, and I don't blame you. But that was a job, not personal.

Not personal? Kidnapping was very personal. I snatched the other chair from Jesse, pushed Jessica out of the way to clear a path, and I was just about to make impersonal contact with the asshole when the chair jerked backward. I went with it, stumbling into David's chest. He wrested the chair from me and set it down.

"Damn it, David. I have every right to kick his ass."

"I'm not going to argue the point, Sugar. I think Grayson is about to tell us that he was undercover for the FBI, and that he tried to keep you as safe as he could without jeopardizing his mission."

This time when Grayson spread his hands, he also shrugged. "Not the FBI, or else Agent Zinn would have found himself in a world of trouble for his unsanctioned mission to apprehend a deep-cover operative."

My brother had accompanied the SAFE Security crew to retrieve Jessica and me when we'd been kidnapped by Grayson Cuyler on behalf of Brick Dixon. The bust had netted him accolades and a promotion.

"Look, I'm not going to apologize. I wouldn't mean it, and you wouldn't believe it." Grayson motioned to the people surrounding us. "And if we weren't above-board, my team would have attempted to blend in. We wanted you to see us. We need your help."

"Explain the khaki." Jessica regarded Cuyler with a fiery scowl. "It's creepy, like cyborg-zombie mutant office workers out for an afternoon stroll to stalk their next victim. I thought government spooks wore suits. You know, so they could be the normal amount of creepy."

The barest trace of amusement curled Cuyler's full lips, and he indulged Jessica. "Everyone would notice suits. There are actually many people here dressed similarly to my colleagues. I chose this uniform with Eastridge and Foraker in mind. I knew you'd spot them. We also weren't sure what time you would arrive. Most people like to hit the flea market early, before the good stuff is gone."

I wasn't worried that he knew where we were going. If he'd been watching us, then he knew that Jessica and I had visited every flea market in the area in the past few weeks, frequently accompanied by David and Jesse. We weren't after the good stuff. We were after deals, and those always came at the last minute. I peeked out from behind David. "SAFE Security wants nothing to do with you, you low-life piece of shit floating on pond scum clinging to lice."

Cuyler chuckled. "Good thing you're not part of the SAFE Security team. Gentlemen, I'd like a private word with the two of you."

Neither David nor Jesse budged. While the trio engaged in a staring contest, I planned out how I'd break the remaining chair over Cuyler's head. I wanted to damage his face. It was far too handsome to belong to a douchebag like him. It needed to be rearranged so that his outsides matched his insides.

Finally Cuyler sighed. "Okay, I guess it won't be private."

A member of the Khaki Club stepped forward, and David shifted me ever so slightly closer to his left side. "Cuyler, are you sure about this? The ladies have not been cleared."

Suddenly I noticed how little of the talking David and Jesse were doing. From my place next to David, I studied him and Jesse. The pair seemed to be aware of all seven adversaries, on alert for the tiniest movement. I took Jessica's hand. "We're going to sit in the truck."

Thankfully Jessica didn't resist when I pulled her with me.

David: Just When You Think You Know Someone

The passenger door to the truck slammed shut, and I relaxed the tiniest bit. Now that Brea and Jessica were out of the direct path of harm should this degenerate into a brawl, I could focus on the immediate threat to me instead of the ways in which Brea might be harmed/cause harm. I was sorely tempted to let her have another go at Gray, but my better sense prevailed. Grayson Cuyler had trained me. He'd picked Dean and me from the sea of hopefuls and trained us for Special Forces.

Once upon a time, I thought I knew everything there was to know about this man. But after our last run-in, I was no longer certain. Seeing Gray was a shock, and for once I was glad that Brea and Jessica were there to shoot off their mouths. They bought me time to calm my fury and assess the situation.

"Is this the kind of job offer we can turn down?"

Gray waved away his entourage and came closer. He was my height, though he sported broader shoulders and thicker muscles. "Not if you value your national security."

"Isn't that your job?" Jesse crossed his arms and rocked back on his heels. To some it might look like he was casually shooting the breeze with two buddies, but I knew the rocking was just his way of stretching his calves—a sort of pre-fight check.

Gray laughed, a short, mirthless burst. "You hear about the hacker that got into the Speaker of the House's personal files?"

That mess had been all over the headlines for months. Every few days, the hacker released embarrassing or classified emails, images, or other documents. I shrugged. "Yeah. So?"

"So the Speaker is just the beginning. This is the warning, the severed finger in a box. The hacker has managed to get some information that's much more sensitive from another important figure." Grayson shrugged. "It's a sensitive matter."

The rage I'd pushed down boiled up again. "You know what else is a sensitive matter? You kidnapped and terrorized my fiancée." I took a step closer, and Jesse didn't stop me.

In fact, he added to my ire. "And her sister."

I poked Gray hard in the chest, driving my fingertip like a stake through his cold, dead heart. "You fucking kidnapped my fiancée."

Gray pressed his lips together, and I knew he was trying not to lose his temper. "At the time, I was under the impression she was just your receptionist. It made sense that you'd hire a former thief, one who had been on our watchlist for almost two decades, to work at SAFE Security. After all, who better than an accomplished con artist to help run the business?"

This raised a red flag in my subconscious, but I didn't have time to pursue it. "I don't appreciate your sarcasm." I may not have originally wanted Brea to be our office manager, but now that she was doing the job, I had to admit that she was damned good at it.

Gray crossed his arms and stood his ground. "That wasn't meant to be tongue-in-cheek, buddy. Someone with her skills—reformed—would be a very valuable asset."

This kind of ass-kissing wasn't Grayson's usual modus operandi. "You're either seriously over-estimating her skills, or underestimating this intense need I have to take a swing at you." In retrospect, it might have been better if Brea had stayed out here with me. At least if I was keeping her from breaking a chair over Grayson's head, then I wasn't fighting the urge to do it myself.

He frowned. "You already took a swing at me. I seem to recall spending a few months recovering from a fractured skull."

That news mollified me the tiniest bit.

Jesse slapped a hand on my shoulder and pulled me back, giving Grayson some space. "The job you're proposing isn't a good fit for our firm."

"You didn't let me finish." Gray flashed the million-dollar smile I had grown to distrust. "We know where the hacker is based—not where the world thinks he is, but where he really is."

"So go get him." When I'd left the military, I'd lost the ability to have blind faith in my government and the people working for them. It seemed the higher up the food chain you went, the more corrupt people were.

"We can't. And truthfully we don't want to. He's sometimes valuable. We just need you to go to San Tesoro, break into his compound, and steal a hard drive. If some of his servers also happened to be destroyed in the process, we wouldn't be upset." Gray motioned to the truck's cab. "Or I can hire those two."

Jesse and I exchanged a glance. Though it lasted a moment and no words were spoken, we had a very substantive conversation. Brea and Jessica might not turn him down, especially if they thought the case would be fun. Jesse pursed his lips, and I let Cuyler in on what we'd decided. "Send the details. We'll get back to you in a week."

"I need you to ship out ASAP."

The ice in Jesse's eyes matched the smoke I was sure steamed from mine. I'd kill Grayson before I let him endanger Brea again. Jesse snarled. "This is the deal. Take it or leave it."

Gray offered his hand, meaning to seal the deal the honorable way. Since this entire exchange was less than honorable, Jesse and I ignored the hand. Jesse picked up the trough and put it in the truck bed, and I did the same with the chair. We secured them with tie-downs, and then we got into the truck.

Jessica was at the steering wheel. She didn't look like she wanted to give up her position, but one look from Jesse had her sliding over. Brea scooted into the back seat, and I joined her there. I texted Dean and Frankie to meet us at SAFE Security headquarters.

We made it to the freeway before Brea poked my arm. "What did he want?"

"He offered us a job." I didn't really want to talk about it with her—not that she wouldn't soon know a lot of the details—but I had other things on my mind. "He said you and Jessica have been on an NEO watchlist for almost twenty years."

Brea blinked.

Jessica twisted around to face me. "He blackmailed you into accepting a job you don't want to do? Don't do this because of us. We're living life by the book now."

Jesse held out his hand to Jessica. "Can I have my wallet back?"

Without missing a beat, she slid it from her bag. "I wasn't going to keep it."

"I know." Jesse tucked his wallet back inside his front jacket pocket.

"I'd planned to slip it back to you later." Jessica somehow managed not to apologize or sound contrite.

"I'm sure you did."

Since Jessica had moved out of the rehab facility and in with our parents, some of her old habits had returned. She'd taken up all manner of artistic endeavors—drawing, painting, and refurbishing furniture. She planned to be an avid jogger, and she liked to drink a glass of wine with dinner. Picking pockets was one of the less desirable traits, and it was impossible to predict what would set it off.

"I always do."

Jesse, for his part, wasn't the least bit upset. I patted my pocket to see if she'd gone after anything of mine, and I caught Brea giving me a strange look.

"What?"

"She won't steal from you or me."

I didn't see how I was different from Jesse, but I knew Jessica had a strict code of honor about not stealing from her sister. I steered the conversation back to Grayson's warning that Brea and Jessica were on a watchlist. "Why would two petty thieves be on an NEO watchlist?"

Brea stared out the window. She'd been kidnapped as a small child and raised to follow in her kidnapper's footsteps—as a thief and a con. "I think a better question is why the NEO would put us on a watchlist instead of returning us to our real parents."

"Yeah," Jessica chimed in. "They knew BS's real kids were in witness protection."

Now Brea regarded me with a frown. "And wouldn't this have come up when you had your buddies in the FBI dig into my past?"

She raised some good points, but the NEO didn't operate in cooperation with other Federal agencies. It's likely that when Keith Rossetti had looked into Brea's past, he would have triggered alarms at the NEO, but he wouldn't have known about it.

Jesse added his two cents. "The NEO would only have watched you if you—or Brian Sullivan—posed a threat to national security. They might not have cared about the rest."

"Or Grayson Cuyler is full of shit." Brea's frown turned to acid. "He was Brick Dixon's hired muscle, and he was sleeping with Dixon's wife—with his full knowledge and consent. I hate that man, and I don't want you working for him."

The factors that would decide whether we took this case would be determined by Dean, Frankie, Jesse, and me. Brea's wishes wouldn't be weighted heavily. This was a business. And now that Cuyler knew Brea was my submissive and my fiancée instead of just a receptionist, he apparently intended to use that leverage to get what he wanted. Right now it was a matter of making sure we had sufficient information so that we didn't get screwed over. If the NEO was hiring out this job, they'd disavow any knowledge of it if the thing went sideways. That also meant we would be on our own.

I didn't mind being on our own. I minded that the NEO potentially had information on Brea about which I was ignorant. And my hands were tied with regard to what I could get from her. I'd nearly destroyed our relationship by digging into her past or insisting she tell me things she wasn't ready to reveal. She had been seeing a therapist for the past six months, but she didn't often come home and share anything from those sessions with me. I wanted to ask, but I'd promised to respect her privacy and her right to tell me things in her own time.

I took Brea's hand, gently sandwiching it between mine. "Sugar, if there's a reason you're on a national security watchlist, I'd like to know. It could be crucial to ensuring your safety and that of my team."

She stared at me, her lips parted and her eyes blinking too quickly. "I don't know. I mean, yeah—I've done stuff. A lot of stuff. But I can't think of anything specific that would endanger national security."

"What about the drug dealers we stole a half million from?" Doubt infused Jessica's question. "That guy did international deals."

I knew about that, though I didn't know many details. I just knew that Brea and/or Jessica had seduced a high-level drug dealer, gained access to his holdings, and cleaned him out. They'd used the money to pay off Eugene Bowen, aka Brian Sullivan, or "BS" as they liked to call him. I generally referred to him by less neutral terms. Anyway, they'd bought themselves a pass out of the criminal lifestyle.

Brea frowned. "I can't see how the NEO would care. They don't enforce drug-related crimes."

"What about that arms dealer BS would do a job for every fall?" Some of the doubt disappeared from Jessica's tone. "I think that guy had links to Russia, and they're evil again."

"Maybe." Brea withdrew her hand from mine, and she balled her fists on her lap. This had nothing to do with me and everything to do with the topic of conversation. "Or those night jobs he'd do when we lived in the Florida Keys? Even when we moved farther north, he'd disappear sometimes for two or three days. Once he was gone for a week."

I didn't want to ask how old they'd been when they'd been left to fend for themselves. But I couldn't stop myself. "He left you alone when you were just kids?"

Brea didn't look concerned or traumatized. "He always left enough food and money for the week. It was like a vacation because he didn't want us out stealing while he was gone. It was during one of those times that we robbed the drug dealer." She unbuckled her seatbelt and slid across the seat. I put my arm around her, and she tucked her head against my shoulder. "Sir, I don't want you to take this job. I don't trust Cuyler at all."

"He trained me." I stroked a caress down her arm. "I know his moves."

She was quick to scowl. "It's been a few years. You both have new moves."

Jesse reached back and patted her knee. "Sugar, there's more to factor into this than the two of you."

I wasn't completely comfortable with his use of my pet name for Brea, but I'd learned to live with it. Jesse and Dean treated her as if she was a little sister, and the nickname had come to mean something altogether innocuous to them. Brea maintained it was their way of bonding with me, even though I'd once punched Jesse for using it. Also because I thought he had a crush on her. It turned out he did not.

She squeezed Jesse's hand before he resumed driving with both hands on the wheel. "I know. I just don't like it. This doesn't feel above-board. There's nothing noble about this mission."

She had a point, but if I were to be honest, there was nothing noble about a lot of our missions. This was no different from when we'd been in the military, only now we weren't lying to ourselves about it. We knew the score going in. We'd protected people's art, meetings, lives, and livelihoods. We'd consulted about security systems and rescued people who'd been kidnapped internationally. Sometimes our missions were noble, but that wasn't a prerequisite.

Jesse pointed to a sign indicating that we were close to Jessica's parents' house. "Am I dropping you home, or are you staying with Brea tonight?"

Though Jessica lived with her parents so they could help her while she recovered from being in a coma for three years, she frequently made use of the guest room in our apartment. I didn't mind, mostly because she tended to be there when I was away on a job.

"Are you kidding? This involves us. We're going with you guys."

Before I could disagree, Brea rested her fingertips on my cheek, subtly urging me to look at her. "Sir, please let us at least sit in on the meeting."

A year ago, I would have denied her outright. But now that I was an enlightened Dom, one who knew that seeking to control too much would drive away my sub, I considered her request. As office manager, she'd sat in on our meetings a few times. She'd even offered valuable suggestions. Jessica was another story. She wasn't technically part of our crew.

At last, I exhaled. "I'm not sure that's my call to make. I'll put it to a vote, Sugar."

She kissed my neck and slid back over to her seat, a satisfied smile on her face, and I knew she was counting on my vote.

It turned out not to matter. Dean and Frankie met us in the lobby of SAFE Security's headquarters, a glorified hallway that Brea and Jessica had redecorated to look like a reception area. It even had three stylish chairs, two small, round tables that Jessica had found at a garage sale and refinished, and the SAFE Security logo painted on the wall in lieu of a painting.

Frankie looked us over, her dark eyes assessing us for invisible damage. Attired in a black evening gown that dipped down pretty low in front and spiky black heels, she took me by surprise. Her short, black hair was styled to frame her face and accent her silky, dark lashes. The only time I'd ever seen her dressed up was when she was undercover and the job required her to assume this kind of role.

"Damn, Frankie. You look hot." Brea whistled as she openly looked my partner up and down. "Sorry we interrupted your date."

This sounds like a stupid guy thing to think, but I was unaware that Frankie went on actual dates. I knew she sometimes went out and that several boyfriends had come and gone over the years, but somehow I never realized that she would wear such feminine clothes and go to dinner or the theater. Seeing Frankie dressed like that was more shocking than being tailed by six government goons and thinly threatened by Cuyler.

"That's okay. Get your asses in the conference room for debrief. Dean and I have been doing research." She turned and headed down the hall like she was wearing her usual combat boots or running shoes and sweats.

Dean was on her heels. Jesse and Jessica wasted no time. As they disappeared down the hall, Brea tugged on my hand. "It looks like she and Dean want all of us in there."

"Yeah." I sucked in my lips as something occurred to me. "When you were waiting in the truck, were you texting with Frankie and Dean?" Otherwise, how would they even know what to research?

"Of course." Brea regarded me as if I'd lost my mind. "I had to make sure you had backup. Frankie seemed to think you and Jesse could handle yourselves. She was right. Also she told me where Jesse hides his guns in the truck. We had your back, Sir."

"So when you asked to be there for the meeting, you already knew you would be."

She shook her head. "I had no idea why she wants me and Jessica in there. We didn't see anything you didn't see."

With dread pooling in the pit of my stomach, I followed Brea into the conference room. The rest of the team had already seated themselves around the long table where we held regular meetings.

Dean put a fresh filter in the coffee maker and set a pot to percolating. "It's great of you to join us. I'm especially relieved you didn't stop in your office to grab a quickie."

Brea sat next to Jessica, and I shot Dean a nasty look as I assumed the seat next to Brea. Sometimes, when I wasn't particularly busy, I'd call Brea into my office for a nooner. The team had learned to knock when my door was closed. "I'd never do that when we had something important to discuss."

Frankie punched up some information on her tablet and cast it to the big screen TV on the wall. "For those who don't know, Grayson Cuyler started off as a Marine. He worked in MARSOC, and he was known for his ability to pick out talent for that branch. About ten years ago, Cuyler disappeared from all records. He showed up as muscle in a few different organized crime syndicates, but he always managed to duck out well before the authorities busted anyone for anything."

"What's MARSOC?" Jessica asked.

I clarified for the non-military person. "United States Marine Corps Forces Special Operations Command. It's part of SOCOM." Before Jessica could ask, I explained further. "Special Operations Command, which is made up of the elite forces of all branches of the military."

Dean went next, elucidating Cuyler's connection to us for Jessica and Brea. "Cuyler selected David and me for MARSOC. David went into ordinance disposal, and I did sharpshooter training. We eventually ended up on a mixed SOCOM team with Jesse and Frankie, both of whom specialized in recon and surveillance. You could say that Grayson Cuyler had a big hand in how our lives turned out."

Brea turned to me. "You never told me that."

"It didn't occur to me. Besides, you had enough shit to deal with." I wished we had snacks. I could do with a cookie or muffin kind of distraction.

With a tiny nod, she accepted my excuse, so I was in the clear for now.

"Guy Rand is the Speaker of the House." Dean pointed at the image Frankie put up. An older man with wrinkly skin, white wisps of hair, and pale, watery blue eyes stared down on us. "He's at war with the extremists in his party, and so every time something new comes out, they're not rushing to his defense. Almost nobody is calling for this hacker's head on a platter, though several agencies are on the case."

Frankie pulled up another slide. This man was middle-aged, spray-tanned, and the vibrancy of his angry eyes leaped from the screen. "Ralph Gorham served on the Armed Services Committee and as the head of the Intelligence Committee while in the Senate. He was voted out of office a few years ago. He spent his time out of the political spotlight building up various business interests around the world, including China and Russia, but now he's been elected President. He's racked up hundreds of accusations of wrongdoing, everything from fraud to corporate malfeasance to using slave labor to build products. We believe his private servers were hacked. Word on the street is that he didn't think hackers would go after something housed in his basement."

Jesse's nose wrinkled with disgust. "Dumbass."

As I had a poor opinion of most world leaders, I didn't comment. "Cuyler wants us to go to San Tesoro, steal the hard drive and destroy whatever we leave behind."

Frankie had more information, but no picture to go with it. "Rumor has it that the NEO feeds information to Carvalho Ferreira Rocha by letting him hack certain servers. They use him to get information out there that would give them an advantage on a national stage."

"No picture?" Jessica cocked her head. "C'mon. Someone must have a picture of him somewhere. I'm assuming this guy is younger?"

"Based on reports of activity going back about fifteen years, we think he's between thirty and sixty." Dean answered. "We only found grainy images that could be of anybody with a medium build, dark hair, and a Hispanic ethnic origin."

"Let's see it." Jesse motioned to the monitor. "Maybe I can clean it up."

Frankie slid a laptop to Jesse, ostensibly with the image in question. He pushed a thumb drive into a port on the computer. A few minutes later, he slid it back to Frankie.

She regarded it thoughtfully. "That's not the same image."

"No. It's Rocha, though. I know a guy."

Frankie projected the image onto the huge monitor. Seconds later, we were looking at a moderately handsome man in his mid-to-late-thirties.

"So it's a snatch and grab." Jessica turned toward Frankie, seemingly unimpressed with the visual. "What risks are involved?"

Frankie clicked on a series of images. They showed Rocha's compound, tucked away in the mountains and dense jungles of San Tesoro. "Accessing the location. There's one way in and one way out." The images weren't terribly clear, and the tree cover could be hiding a lot of problems.

"Security." Brea chimed in. "A place like that will have at least twelve armed guards at any given time, maybe more if they think an attack is imminent. Taking that place by force is going to be extremely difficult. You might be better off with infiltration."

I saw where this was headed, and now I understood why Grayson would consider asking Brea and Jessica to do this job. "There's no way in hell you're going down there, Sugar. You don't have the training or experience."

She sat back and didn't argue.

"Are you kidding me?" Jessica sputtered. She looked to Brea, silently imploring her support, but Brea didn't meet her sister's eyes. "Maybe we don't have much experience with storming a place, but we've spent our lives learning to infiltrate. I speak fluent Spanish. Brea knows enough to get by."

This didn't jive with what Brea had told me about her past. "The petty stuff you've done doesn't prepare you for something like this."

She turned her slashed brows in Brea's direction, but she said nothing further.

Now I was dying to know what Brea hadn't told me that Jessica knew. "Sugar? Is there something you want to say?"

Brea fastened her gaze on the steel gray table top. "I haven't spoken Spanish in years."

That wasn't what I'd meant. "Anything else?"

This time she lifted her gaze and met mine. Misery stained the depths of her emerald eyes. "BS always had a long con in mind whenever he moved us somewhere. Sometimes Jessica and I were part of the plan, so yes, we have experience with infiltration. Still, Sir, I agree with you that it doesn't prepare us for something like this. Perhaps you feel that your training has prepared you, but I don't want you to go either." She slowly panned the room, making eye contact with Frankie, Dean, and Jesse. "I don't want any of you to go. This whole deal smells bad."

"I agree," Dean said. "But I know Grayson Cuyler. One way or another, he's going to get what he wants. I'd rather control my part than have it dictated to me."

"What's the worst that can happen if Ralph Gorham's private business dealings become public?" Brea appealed to Dean. "He gets investigated? Prosecuted? Removed from office? Who cares?"

Dean pointed to the images of Rocha that Frankie had put back up. "That guy could have classified information that could put lives at risk, destroy the economy, or take down the whole government. He's not a good guy."

"He doesn't seem that bad." Brea glanced at the monitor briefly before focusing on Dean. "He looks like a nerd, a tech geek who enjoys hacking and long walks on the beach. I bet he's lonely, and he'd be easy to infiltrate. Frankie could do it. I mean, look at her. She's smoking hot. Even I'm thinking of changing lanes."

I'd seen Brea check out both Jesse and Dean, but she'd never made a comment like that before about either of them. I was more than a little shocked, but I covered it up by wagging my finger at Frankie. "Don't you start calling her 'Sugar' too."

"It never crossed my mind." Frankie didn't appear impressed by Brea's compliment. "However she may have a point about infiltration. I could pose as a wealthy heiress, Jesse and Dean could be my bodyguards, and David could be my gay assistant."

"Why would I have to be gay?"

Brea smacked my arm with the back of her hand. "Silly. If you're not, then you're competition. If Rocha is going to fall for Frankie, then he needs to know she isn't playing Hide the Sausage with her secretary."

That kind of plan seemed like it could take months, and that was only if Rocha took the bait. Frankie would be a catch for any man, but that didn't mean Rocha was fishing. "What if he doesn't like women?"

Frankie laughed, the husky sound filling the room. "Then it's fortunate I'll have a gay assistant. Let Dean do your eyebrows."

"Carvalho's not gay," Jessica said.

"You don't know that." Dean sat forward, his hands steepled on the table. "I'll get you an appointment at my salon. You might as well get a manicure and your hair styled. Will you be wearing a bathing suit? I'll sign you up for a wax too."

"No way," Brea scoffed. "I like his happy trail. It's sexy. Though I wouldn't object to some trimming and manscaping."

"He's not gay," Jessica repeated. This time she slapped her hand on the table. "I know this for a fact."

Brea's gaze dropped to her lap.

"Care to explain?" Jesse rested his elbows on the table and clasped his hands together. I knew the caliber of questions running through his brain. I also recognized the Dom tone he was using. He wasn't giving her a choice in the matter.

Jessica seemed nonplussed. "I met him a long time ago. His dad is an arms dealer who was friends with BS. Of course, he wasn't going by Carvalho Rocha back then. We called him Charlie Ferrari. As he was fond of saying, he liked fast cars and even faster women."

Brea kicked her under the table, so Jessica stopped talking.

I looked from Brea to Jessica and back. "Sugar, is there anything you need to tell me? What's the real reason you don't want me going down to San Tesoro?"

Jessica coughed. "Jeeze. Enough with the intrigue. Charlie was a target. His old man screwed BS over on a deal one time, and so BS wanted revenge."

"Charlie liked me," Brea said quietly. "So I flirted with him and pumped him for information BS could use to get back at his dad. It worked, though BS didn't make money from the deal. He didn't care because Charlie's father lost everything." She turned to me, her emerald eyes wide as she begged for understanding. "Sir, he's not a bad person. He's all bark and no bite, really quite submissive."

I tried not to think about how that admission and the things she'd done to me that morning were linked, and so I threw my brain at other avenues. Looking to Jesse, I sought support. Guy support—not like a jock strap, though. This was more emotional. "So when Gray said that he might send Brea and Jessica, he must have already known they were acquainted."

Jessica let loose a short burst of laughter. "But not the details. Brea broke his heart, left him crying in his own drunken vomit. He won't want to see either of us again. It's best if Frankie goes."

Unwilling to hang Frankie out like that, I shook my head. "I'm voting for covert action. We sneak in, grab what we need, and leave. Nobody needs to know we were there. The forest provides cover for Rocha, but it will also provide cover for us. We've done ops like this before. It'll take four days, tops. That includes travel, surveillance, and planning."

Dean nodded. "That's the most expedient way to handle this. We have other jobs scheduled. Brea, I'm going to need you to do some juggling. The four of us will need to go to San Tesoro together."

"Sure thing." Brea pressed her lips together. "Or you could just tell Grayson Cuyler to fuck off. I'd be willing to take another swing at him for good measure."

Jesse spread his hands. "I'm willing to tell him to fuck off, and I'll also buy a pair of brass knuckles so Sugar doesn't hurt her fist too much."

Brea grinned. "That's thoughtful, but I was going to use a sledge hammer."

Jesse's smile matched Brea's. "Even better. We have one in the tool closet."

The two of them would do this all night if I let them. "That's two votes for covert action and one for not accepting the mission. Frankie?"

She sighed. "I'm with Jesse. Let the NEO or the CIA handle this. It's not our thing. Tell Cuyler to fuck off, though I'm not in favor of arming Brea. Despite her bragging, she doesn't actually like to hit people. She still pulls her punches during our training workouts."

"That's because I like you." Brea turned her flirty grin on Frankie. "I don't like Cuyler. He's ass cheese."

It looked like the mission was not going forward. I nailed Jessica and Brea with a firm stare. "Neither of you will pursue this matter."

Jessica snorted. "As if. We're treasure hunters now."

I swallowed my crack about their propensity for hunting for treasure at flea markets because, all-in-all, I preferred them engaging in that kind of pursuit. Still I prompted Brea. "Sugar?"

"I definitely won't pursue the matter, but I make no promises when it comes to Cuyler. If I see him, I may not be able to control my reflexes." She followed up with that devilish smile I loved so well.

We ordered takeout for the six of us, and then we broke the news to Grayson via text message. On the way home, Brea reached across the console for my hand.

Michele Zurlo

"Sir?"

She'd used my title a couple of times tonight. I couldn't tell if she was feeling submissive or trying to placate me. "Yes?"

"About Charlie...It was a long time ago."

I took my eyes from the road to glance at her briefly. "It's okay, Sugar. We both have exes."

She was quiet for several blocks, during which I held her hand. Then she sighed, the kind of sigh that says much more than words could. "He's not an ex. He was a mark. I remember how upset you got the last time I told you about seducing a mark."

I'd wondered if the drug dealer was the only time she'd done something like that. I had no stones to throw. I'd seduced my way into the lives of targets before. The difference lay in the fact that I made the choice to run the op that way, and I was pretty sure Brea hadn't been given much of a choice. I squeezed her hand. "I'm sorry, Sugar. I just hate that BS used you like that. If he was alive right now, I'd probably kill him."

"He never pressured me. He used to pressure Jessica, though." More blocks passed. Streetlights chased regular shadows from the car. When she spoke again, she sounded utterly defeated. "Maybe I took on the job because I wanted to save her from having to do it."

Seriously, if the man were in front of my car, I'd run him over, back up, and run him over again. Then I'd get out of the car and beat his carcass until he was unrecognizable. I was pissed for both Brea and Jessica. Nobody deserved to be used like that.

Brea: Matters of the Heart

I could tell by the way David was driving that he was livid. When he got mad at me for doing or saying something, I was usually equally angry with him. We shouted, argued, and sometimes I threw things in his general direction. That didn't bother me in the least. This, however—this bothered me.

The drive home didn't take long. David pulled into his parking spot and killed the engine. I turned to face him. "Please don't be angry with me. I did what I had to do."

He pounded his fist on the wheel. "I'm not angry at you. I'm angry because you had to do it. Nobody should have to prostitute themselves in order to get information for a con man."

"It wasn't like that." On the surface, perhaps it had been, but beneath it was the first man I'd topped, the first man who'd knelt for me, who'd submitted to me. "Charlie and I liked each other. I didn't want to break his heart. He's wasn't a bad person. He was sweet." In some ways, he'd been my first love—not that I really knew anything about love back then.

David unfurled his fist and looked at me. Misery mixed with bitterness and anger, coloring his eyes a muddy brown. "Would you have seduced him if BS hadn't made you?"

I shrugged, though I knew the answer.

He wasn't going to let me off that easily. "Brea, answer me."

"I wouldn't have seduced him, but I probably would have slept with him eventually."

David seemed to accept that, though it didn't make him less furious. "How old were you?"

"Sixteen, almost seventeen." The moment I said it, I closed my eyes. Until a year ago, I'd been under the impression I was older than I actually was. If I'd thought I was sixteen, then I'd been fifteen. I knew

David had arrived at the same conclusion. "He wasn't my first boyfriend." I didn't want to tell him that most of my boyfriends had been marks.

David leaned his head against his seat and stared at the roof of the car. "The more you tell me about your past, the more in awe I am that you are not completely fucked up."

I huffed out a chuckle-snort. "That's open to debate."

"You're strong." He murmured, more to himself than to me. "Resilient, funny, smart, complex, fearless, generous, tenderhearted— utterly beautiful."

"I'm not going to argue with compliments."

"Good. I'd spank your ass."

He'd let go of my hand when he'd pulled into the parking garage. I reached over and took his again. "Sir, I'd really like if you spanked me tonight."

His gaze moved slowly across the ceiling before falling to meet mine. "Do you feel like you need to SAM?"

I was a smart-assed masochist sometimes, meaning I liked to smart off to him while he spanked or flogged me. It was how I let off steam and goaded him to keep going or hit harder. Right now, I wasn't feeling angry enough to do that. Mostly I felt sad that he was so furious on my behalf and afraid that we hadn't heard the last of Grayson Cuyler. "No, Sir. I don't want to SAM tonight."

"Okay. I'll spank you, but I choose the aftercare."

I could live with that. He held my hand all the way to the apartment. I didn't know why talking about Charlie swirled a complicated emotional response. I felt guilty for the way I'd treated Charlie, a man who hadn't crossed my mind until Jesse had found that picture. I felt bad because David was angry and hurting for me. And deep down, there was more, but I couldn't catch the emotions to name them. I definitely knew what I'd be discussing with Nikki Eliachevsky, my therapist, this week.

We barely spoke as we entered the apartment and took care of basic tasks—sorting the mail, using the bathroom, undressing. David pointed to my kneeling pillows stacked next to the fireplace, and I obeyed the silent order. He disappeared into the bedroom, while I grabbed the top pillow and set it on the floor in front of the sofa. Then I knelt, my spine straight and my hands, open with the palms facing up, resting on my knees.

When he returned to the living room, he paused, and I knew he was looking at me, soaking in the visual evidence of my submission and using it to feed his Dominant side.

After forever had passed, he took his place in the center of the sofa. "Sugar, what's going to happen right now?"

"You're going to spank me, Sir."

"Why?"

I hadn't misbehaved, and this wasn't for his pleasure. Because the question didn't fit the usual responses, it threw me off, and my answer wasn't prompt.

"Sugar?"

"Sorry, Sir. You're spanking me because I asked you to."

"And why did you ask me to spank you?"

I hated that he was pushing me to think beyond the basic need. I cast around my brain for an adequate reason. "Because I can't make this sick feeling go away."

"Sick feeling?"

"Yes, Sir. I don't know exactly how to describe it."

"Dread? Guilt? Shame?"

Maybe it was a little bit of all those, but I wasn't ready to dig deeper. "Sadness." My vocal cords barely worked, and I had almost no volume.

"What caused the sadness?"

I was glad this position meant my gaze was riveted to the floor just in front of my knees. "There are some things about my past that I don't want you to know."

His fingertips pressed into his thigh. I caught the tense move from the periphery of my vision. "Why not?"

This part was less difficult because I'd discussed it several times with Nikki. "Because those things are in the past, and I want them to stay there. If you know them, then it's always there, polluting your mind and the way you think of me."

"I love you, Sugar. There's nothing you can tell me that's going to change the way I feel about you. I want to know everything there is to know about you, but I'm willing to wait. I'm not going anywhere for a good number of years, and neither are you." He touched my hair, pushing it back from my face and caressing me at the same time.

I didn't argue his point. Confident people had a way of making blanket statements that they truly wanted to believe. I was sure that if David ever found out everything in my past, he'd never look at me the same way again. He might continue to love me. He might abide by his promise to remain by my side for the rest of our lives. But there would always be a hesitation—just enough to let me know that what I'd told him had fractured his love.

He touched my hair and face. I closed my eyes and gave myself over to his affectionate caresses. Some of the sick feeling in the pit of my stomach eased.

He placed one of the throw pillows on his lap. "Come on up, Sugar."

This was his favorite position for spanking me. It was comfortable for us both. I arranged myself across his lap with my knees underneath me and my ass lifted. The pillow he'd put on his lap took some of the stress off my knees and allowed me to maintain my position longer.

Immediately I felt the roughness of his palm against my posterior. It moved in circles, stimulating me in unexpected ways. Normally before a spanking I was a bundle of nerves, but not this time. Or maybe I was strung so tightly that the slightest touch was magnified. By the time his forays spread to my upper thighs, the small moan in my throat deepened and defied containment.

He started lightly, warming up his hand and my bottom. Soon the force doubled, and doubled again. As I cried out, I became aware of tears wetting my cheeks. Blows rained across both cheeks and my upper thighs. A few caught my pussy, and each time, my ass lifted higher to give him better access.

My ass was on fire, but I didn't want him to stop. I begged him for more, and he didn't let up. Now the blows centered more and more around my pussy. All of a sudden, a climax detonated in my core. Sounds of pleasure mixed with misery. Tears dripped from my eyes, and the languor of orgasm calmed my insides.

Sir picked me up and turned me around. He wrapped a soft blanket around me and cradled me in his warm embrace. "You did wonderfully, Sugar. That was a beautiful climax. Thank you for giving yourself to me, for trusting me to make sure you got what you needed. I love you so much."

He talked to me, whispers and murmurs of praise and affection, until my sobs had quieted. I clung to him, my anchor in this maelstrom.

Later he made hot chocolate, and we snuggled on the sofa while watching Charade.

After a lazy Sunday filled with slow lovemaking and lots of cuddling, I was ready to return to work Monday morning. I spent a few hours in SAFE Security's offices making sure everyone's travel arrangements and paperwork were correct. Dean and Jesse had a job in Seattle, while Frankie and David were scheduled to be in Atlanta by nightfall. As Jesse had warned me, Dean and David weren't very good about filing reports or turning in receipts. I'd developed a system that required them to start the paperwork before they left so that when they returned, they only needed to finish it. Yeah, there was a lot to finish, but I found it easier to get them to actually do it if they'd already begun it.

By mid-morning, I'd completed what I needed to finish for the day, so I went downstairs to the storefront Jessica and I were renting for our treasure museum and/or reclaimed furniture shop. I didn't know where she was going with this furniture thing, but I didn't voice an objection. If this made her happy, then I wanted to support the path she'd chosen.

However I didn't really love it. Though finding Alf Bolin's treasure had been a harrowing experience because I'd been kidnapped and forced into a precarious situation, it had also been wildly exciting. I wanted to find another treasure, so I'd been researching a few. I'd narrowed it down to hidden gold mines in Colorado and northern Missouri. Neither of these had gold in them, but they marked places nearby were loot was purported to be buried.

When Jessica sailed in a few minutes later, I had the map and details of the first legend on my laptop screen. Our shop was divided into two parts. The showroom had displays of our treasure—including the large clockwork tasked with counting down to a fatal detonation, and the vault door from the cave—and a few pieces that Jessica had finished. I'd helped her with them, but not a lot. While I was good with mechanics and building, she had the artist's eye, so the detail work and finishes were all hers.

The other part was where the transformations happened. This was where we cleaned and researched the different items we'd found in the vault. It was also where Jessica's workshop was located. I'm not sure the store was zoned for the kind of work she did, but our landlords didn't complain.

She threw her bag on a work table littered with tools and pieces of a window frame she'd disassembled. Her hair was much shorter than it had been Saturday. Gone were her long brown locks that were the same as mine. She'd shorn them into a pixie cut that looked exceptionally cute on her. It brought out her green eyes and emphasized the sharpness of her cheekbones.

"I love your hair." I ran my fingers through it to see if I could get a few curls to stand up.

She must have known my intention because she stopped me after one run-through. "Thanks. I wanted something different."

"It's different. And sexy."

She stuck her hip out in a mock suggestive pose. "Do you think the boys will like it? I've had my eye on Danny Walsh in particular."

"Who's Danny Walsh?" Jesse came in, a trough in one hand and a chair in the other. He set them down in the middle of the floor and perched his hands on his hips.

Jessica tapped a fingertip to his lips. "Wouldn't you like to know?" She burst into giggles before she finished her sentence.

I didn't see what was so funny. I had no idea who Danny Walsh was either. Jesse lifted a questioning brow in my direction, but I merely shrugged. "Thanks for bringing our stuff. I'm not sure what Jessica is going to do with one chair, though. David should have let me smash it over Cuyler's head."

"He was worried the rest of the NEO agents would arrest you for assaulting a government asshole. I was relieved when the two of you got into my truck." He faced Jessica again, but this time he nailed her with a firm look. "Who is Danny Walsh?"

She rolled her eyes and flounced away from Jesse. "Legendary smuggler during the Prohibition. He was handsome and dashing, totally exciting and completely outside the law."

Now it was coming back to me. She'd gone through a few years where she'd research an infamous criminal—the romantic ones, not the murderous or cruel ones—and talk about him as if they'd actually met. Once she'd met someone who'd worked on a bootlegging vessel, but he'd been so old that his papery skin had been almost translucent.

Jesse frowned, but he didn't respond directly. "I'll be right back."

Once he had left the store, I turned to Jessica. "It's been a long time since you've talked about your old bootlegger boyfriends."

Moments passed as she stared at me and played her lower lip between her teeth. Then she pressed her lips together. "They were always easier to deal with than real life. Fake guys will do or say anything I need them to."

I felt the weight of something big fall from her admission, but before I could catch it, Jesse came back. He carried a huge steamer trunk, hefted onto his shoulder as if it weighed nothing. I recognized the decoupage trunk over which Jessica and I had discussed the agents tailing us.

He set it down next to the chair. "I picked this up too. You said you guys had one growing up."

We hadn't owned much of anything growing up, not for long. Possessions had come in and out of our life, and we'd learned early not to get too attached to anything. Jesse knew this already. The gift puzzled me. He'd gone all the way back to the flea market, probably by himself, to buy a trunk because we'd linked it to a childhood memory?

"I couldn't find a tea set to put inside, but I did find a few books."

Jessica opened the lid, and I came closer to peer inside. The authors were unfamiliar to me, but the titles said enough. There were biographies of all manner of people, from Benjamin Franklin to Claudette Colvin to Lewis and Clark. Some titles weren't obvious, like *Hope Leslie*. Was that a person?

I preferred to read fiction. Jessica was the one who went for nonfiction, particularly historical nonfiction. It occurred to me that the trunk and the books were meant for Jessica. I stepped back to get a better look at my two companions.

Jesse watched Jessica, his pale blue eyes darting from my sister to the trunk and back. He was nervous, though he was careful to disguise most of his tells. He didn't suck his upper lip, tug at his ear, or run his hands over his very short hair. He didn't fidget, and no worry lines creased his brow.

For her part, Jessica appeared mildly surprised with the gift. She rooted through the titles and scanned the backs of a few. The books appeared new, not something he'd picked up at the flea market.

Finally Jesse ran his hand over his head. "I've got some work to do, so I'm going to get going."

Jessica looked up, flashing her brightest and flirtiest smile. "Thanks. This is awesome. Once I scrape the decoupage off this thing and we see what's underneath, then I'll figure out what to make out of it."

Jesse opened his mouth to say something, but in the end, he just nodded. "I'll see you both later."

I watched him go, and part of me wanted to go after him and give him a hug.

"Blackbeard." Jessica had been crouching, but now she sat all the way down on the floor and opened to the first page. "Now there was an interesting person. Give him a shave, and he can be my next boyfriend. And when I get tired of him, I can share him with my friends like he did with his wife."

"Jessica, I think Jesse has a crush on you."

She snorted, a derisive noise that said quite clearly that she disagreed.

"No, really. He got that trunk for you. You were the one who said we had one in New Jersey, not me. You were the one who sounded nostalgic about it."

She waved it all away. "It was all made up. I wanted to talk to you about the tails we'd picked up."

"I know that, but Jessica—he didn't. Not only did he get you the trunk, but he filled it with books you'd like."

Her only response was a dry chuckle and an eye roll.

"Jessica, I'm serious."

"I can see that." She got up and tossed the book back into the trunk. "Do you want me to give it back?"

Whether she liked him back or not, Jesse wouldn't want the gift returned. "I want you to stop flirting with him."

"Oh, please. He knows it's not serious. Besides, you have no room to talk." She crossed to her work table and rummaged through the tools piled there.

I knew I flirted a lot. It was a leftover habit from when I'd been out to manipulate every person I'd met. David had commented on it a couple of times, and I'd worked to rein it in. "When you both know it's not serious, flirting is okay. I think Jesse is starting to take you seriously, and you do flirt with him a lot more than with Dean or David."

She shrugged. "He knows it's not serious. This is probably just because we did sexual things last night."

Shock ran through me, though in retrospect I shouldn't have been surprised. Jessica and I were raised to use people, especially men, to get what we wanted. Though the trail of my past was littered with a lot of short, shallow relationships, Jessica's was strewn with barbed wire and broken glass. Men were a means to an end for her—they were fun until she was finished with them, or—more often—they were marks until she got what she wanted and moved on.

"Here it is." She lifted the heat gun. "Now I'll find out what's under all that hideous paste and pictures of flowers."

I wasn't willing to change the topic. "Jesse wouldn't have slept with you unless he meant it. He might date a lot, but he knows that you're different."

She shot me a sour look as she headed back to the trunk. "Because I'm your sister? Get over yourself, will ya? He knew it was just for kicks—both times. I made it perfectly clear that it was just exercise, and he was great about giving me a pity fuck. Let me tell you—my stamina isn't what it used to be, but I'm working on it."

I had no words. Jessica unloaded the trunk, plugged in her heat gun, and set to work scraping the trunk down to the original finish.

What could I say to make her understand that Jesse wasn't like the other men she'd dated/used? Underneath that gruff and silent exterior, he was kind and funny, and he had a good heart. I watched her for a little while as my conscience nagged at me. Finally I gave in. "David's been working all morning. I'm going to run up and see if he's ready for a break."

She grinned. "You do that."

I didn't go directly to David's office. Instead I found myself hovering outside Jesse's office, gathering the courage to knock. The door was open, but he'd set up his desks to face two walls covered in screens. Three of them were on right now, and Jesse's fingers flew over two different keyboards.

My courage and conscience warred. One wanted to back away and let the chips fall where they may. The other blared a siren in my ears that reminded me about all the ways in which Jesse had been a good friend to me. My courage—or lack thereof—argued that Jesse was David's friend, and that I should have David talk to Jesse. In the end, my conscience won. Or, at least it made me knock on the opened door.

Jesse swiveled around, a frown marring his chin. When his gaze landed on me, the frown deepened. "Sugar? Is everything okay?"

"Can I talk to you?"

"Yeah, sure. Come on in."

I closed the door, which set off some kind of 'bro' alarm in Jesse because he popped out of his chair. I held up a hand. "Nobody's in trouble. Don't worry; this has nothing to do with David."

He sank back down. "Okay. Have a seat. What's on your mind?"

Like the other offices, Jesse's had a sofa because sometimes they slept there. It was the nature of the job. I was too nervous to sit down. Instead I wringed my hands together and paced the width of the room. Jesse watched me, wariness etching tiny lines around his mouth.

Finally I took a deep breath and faced him. "Jesse, I love you."

Color drained from his face, and he froze in place. "Brea, that's kind of sudden."

I stared at him, waiting for my brain to figure out what he meant. Finally I got it. "Not like that. I love you as a friend."

Most of his color returned, as did his bright smile and infectious chuckle. "Okay—*that*, I can handle. I also love you as a friend."

"I know, which is why I have to warn you about Jessica."

He sobered up instantly, and he didn't pretend to not know what I was talking about. "Why? You think I can't handle myself?"

I wasn't about to let him stop me. "I don't know why I didn't notice it before today. Maybe I thought you were just being nice to my sister because she's important to me. But you like her. You're attracted to her."

At this point, I paused to check his reaction. He lifted a shoulder. A shrug was such a noncommittal move. It could mean anything. I interpreted it as an admission of sorts.

"Jesse, she's not serious about you. She's never going to be serious about you."

"You don't know that." He folded his hands on his lap and regarded me with a mild scowl.

As sure as I knew David would eat a plate full of cupcakes if I left them out, I knew that Jessica would never be serious about Jesse or any other man. It was the way she was raised. The first two years after we'd left BS, neither of us dated seriously. We both used men for whatever we wanted—dinner, a movie, sex. Sometimes we wanted companionship, and so we targeted men with that aim in mind.

The difference for me was that I had three years without Jessica whispering in my ear about how men and romantic relationships had limited value and expiration dates. And I had David, who had come along when I was ready to take a chance on something more. Of course I'd done that because the relationship had come with a built-in expiration date. He'd captured my heart, and he'd repeatedly refused to let me sabotage our love.

Jessica didn't have that time. As the embodiment of the voice of cynicism and doubt, she had no intention of changing her position on relationships and the value of men. The happiness she'd recently found was easily shattered, and there was no way in hell she was going to let a man get emotionally close to her. As much as she was giving Sylvia and Warren—the parents from whom BS had abducted us—a chance, she was definitely letting Sylvia in while keeping things superficial with Warren.

"Jesse, it's not personal. She thinks you pity her and that you understand it's not serious." I went to him, knelt down on the floor, and took his hands in mine. It wasn't kneeling like I did with David. This was purely for logistical purposes. "I love my sister, and I know exactly who she is."

He sighed and squeezed my hands. "She made it clear that it wasn't serious."

I'd believed what Jessica had told me. She had no reason to lie. But I didn't believe Jesse accepted the situation. "I know you better than she does. I know you're not the kind of man who'd screw around with my sister if you weren't serious. I just don't want to see you hurt. She'll break your heart if you let her."

"I'll be careful." He stroked my hair back from my face and kissed my forehead.

"Jesse—" The door burst open, and Dean barged in. A big guy with bulky muscles that he hid behind designer suits and sweater vests, he still managed to be imposing—especially when he regarded us with a menacing frown. "What's going on?"

I rocked back and rose to my feet. "We're talking."

"About?" His perfectly groomed eyebrows drew together, two vicious brown slants accenting dark green eyes.

"About none of your business." Unimpressed with Dean's bluster, Jesse stood and parked his hands on his hips. "What did you need?"

Dean took a step in my direction, trying to intimidate me with his Dom-ly presence. "Sugar?"

I closed the space and cupped his cheeks in my hands. "Emotions. Relationships. What kind of woman Jesse should settle down with. Did you have an opinion you'd like to share?"

The imposing frown and slanted eyebrows disappeared. Dean drew back. "Hell, no. Sugar, you can't make someone settle down. They have to want it. Not everybody is as willing to be whipped like David is."

I couldn't summon a smile or a laugh at Dean's dig at how I'd domesticated David because I was too worried about Jesse. I turned back to Jesse. "Sometimes careful isn't enough."

He nodded somberly. "Noted."

David: Some People Won't Go Away

Brea and I had driven to the office separately. She planned to work in the treasure museum, which they still hadn't named, and I planned to try out a new ropes course with Dean that was about an hour outside of town.

The morning flew past smoothly, which worried me. I knew Grayson Cuyler too well to think he'd let us refuse the job with just a text. Even a phone call wouldn't have done the trick. When the buzzer on the elevator sounded just after Brea went downstairs, I knew who was on the other side before I checked the camera feed. At least he'd come alone.

He wore a wide grin and a sharp suit, and he sailed into SAFE Security as if he owned the place. I remembered the first time I set eyes on Grayson Cuyler. He'd been watching training exercises for new Marine recruits. He exuded confidence and an air of mystery; I'd been drawn to him because I'd wanted very much to be like him.

Fast forward fifteen years, and I couldn't help but still be a little in awe of the man who'd made my career.

He offered his hand, but I didn't take the bait. Cuyler played to win, and his cocky smile didn't admit defeat.

I glanced at his hand, and then I looked directly into his eyes. "What do you want?"

"To talk. I didn't like the text you sent Saturday. It was so impersonal and abrupt."

"No, thanks." That's all my text had said, and I repeated it now. "We're not interested in working for you."

"The lobby looks fantastic." Gray checked out our new and improved lobby, which we'd remodeled after he and his team of thugs had shot it up. Jessica had even painted our logo on one wall in metallic silver paint. Cuyler gestured to the hallway that led to my office. "I have sensitive information to share with you. Shall we?"

Dean and Frankie were working out in our third floor gym, and Jesse was in his office, which was down the opposite hall from mine. "Let me assemble the team."

Gray put his hand on my arm, power radiating from his grip. "I'd rather just the two of us have a private conversation. It won't take long." Then he held up his hands. "I promise, I'm minimally armed."

At one point, I'd trusted this man with my life, but now all bets were off, and not because he was minimally armed. Like me, the man was lethal without a weapon. Still I shrugged off my misgivings and led him to my office. He extracted a manila file folder from under his jacket and threw it on my desk. Then he stuck his hands in his pockets, a casual pose that meant he was waiting on me.

I sat in my chair and opened the file. It contained eight-by-ten glossies. The top one showed a much younger Brea deep in conversation with an older man wearing wire-rimmed glasses. He looked familiar, but his name didn't come to me. The next one was a satellite image that showed her in some kind of compound, a rifle slung over her shoulder. The third featured a swarthy man kissing her cheek, and the last two showed her speaking with groups of people. I picked out a known gun runner, two high-level drug dealers, and Eugene Bowen, the kidnapper she'd known as Brian Sullivan.

I closed the file folder. "What's all this?"

"This is the woman you're planning to marry. Are you aware of her background?"

While I knew a lot about her background, there was a ton that was still a mystery. For the most part, Brea didn't like to talk about her past. She had secrets and things she just didn't want to talk about, and I'd promised to respect her wishes. I lifted my shoulder in a noncommittal move. It was the ultimate passive-aggressive evasive maneuver.

Grayson chuckled. "I have to be honest, David. I never thought you'd be blinded by love. It's kind of sweet." He perched on the arm of the chair on the other side of my desk. "I looked into how the two of you met. The FBI agents with whom you worked filed reports, and I followed up with phone calls. Liam Adair and Keith Rossetti were quick to come to Brea's defense, and that's when I realized that she was a master con artist."

Verbal games and intrigue weren't funny when they involved my fiancée. "I'm aware of her past, as are you. Cut the bullshit and tell me why you came. I'm not changing my mind about the mission."

"Fair enough." He got to his feet, opened the file folder, and tapped his thumb on the older, bespectacled man speaking to a teenaged Brea. "That's Luis Ramirez, wanted for smuggling drugs and arms in sixteen countries. He's involved with human trafficking and efforts to arm home-grown insurgents in the US." He flipped to the next picture. "This is a training facility for a Columbian drug cartel."

I dismissed them both. "She's never been to Columbia." Of course I had no way of knowing if she had or not. In her secret box that she kept hidden from even me, I knew she had a stack of fake driver's licenses and passports.

This time, Gray did the shrugging. "Associating with many of these people is treason. I don't even have to arrest her or charge her with anything. There won't be a trial. She has sensitive information that we need for purposes of national security. I can lock her in a cell in a black site and throw away the key."

Cold fingers of rage wrapped around my vital organs. I rose slowly, facing my former CO, and it took every ounce of self-control not to kill him. Even if the photos weren't real, I had no doubt that Gray would follow through on his threat because he believed in violence and retribution. "You unbelievable bastard. What the fuck happened to you? You didn't used to be such a supreme asshole."

Gray's smile reappeared. "In my position, you'd do the same. You'd find a weakness and exploit it. I've always admired you for how well you learned that lesson."

Yeah, I had been a damned fine soldier until I'd started asking questions. The military didn't like people who questioned orders, and I'd left rather than work blindly. It just wasn't who I was. "I would never use an innocent person as a pawn."

"There's no such thing as innocence." Cuyler sank into the chair and studied me through shrewd, dark gray eyes. "I could ask what's happened to you, David. You used to be one of my best."

Fire seared my chest, rising up and threatening to boil over. I leaned forward. "Are you fucking serious?"

He shook his head as if he'd done his best and I was the wayward child who didn't listen to reason. "You were dishonorably discharged for failing to follow orders."

The rage boiled over. I leaped over my desk, grabbed Cuyler by his shirt, and hauled him from the chair. He didn't resist, not even when I shook him. "If refusing to bomb a tiny village comprised of women and children makes me dishonorable, then I gladly claim the title."

"There was more going on in that place than you could see. If I've told you once, I've told you a thousand times—a soldier's job is to carry out orders without question. The people giving the orders know a hell of a lot more than you." With a neat martial arts move that I saw coming and allowed to happen, he broke my hold and straightened his jacket.

"I'm not a murderer."

Gray snorted. "You've killed plenty of people, whether you were carrying out missions for the US government or for your clients, people have died at your hands. Why, just a few months ago in this very building, you took four lives."

Four lives that wouldn't have been lost if Gray hadn't orchestrated an attack on my building. I threw a punch, which Gray saw coming and blocked with his elbow, and so I followed with a vicious left hook. Since he didn't block, I figured he hadn't anticipated it. Using a move Frankie had taught me, I followed up with a swift jab to his midsection, and then I put distance between us. If he came after me, I'd gladly spatter this office with his insides.

But he merely wiped the blood from his lip and laughed. "Glad to see you've still got fire in your belly. You're going to need it for this."

"You used to care about protecting people." It killed me to see my mentor in this horrific light, and the fact that he threatened the woman I loved only made it worse.

"I care about protecting this country and her citizens—by any means necessary. If that means a few so-called innocents lose their lives, then so be it. I can live with my actions because I'm doing this for the greater good." Gray tossed a second file folder on my desk. This one was thicker. I opened it to find a dossier on Carvalho Ferreira Rocha. "This is everything we know, which isn't as much as we'd like to know. It's urgent that this matter is resolved before next Wednesday. At midnight in three days, Rocha plans to release information that could endanger the lives of millions."

Trapped in this nightmare, I tapped the file. "How do I know you won't still go after Brea?"

He looked me straight in the eye. "You have my word."

I didn't believe him, but what could I do? One thing was for sure— I was going to go after Grayson Cuyler until all records of Brea's past were permanently destroyed.

"If it makes you feel any better, know that I admire your choice in a life partner. She's smart and sassy, and she has the heart of a warrior. And so do you." He took a step toward the door, and then he turned back. "David, I need you for this. You're the only one I trust to carry out this mission."

Bullshit. "Why not ask your contacts in organized crime to take out Rocha?" He'd somehow made it look as if his freedom was due to a technicality, and so his contacts still considered him a friend.

Grayson's smile dimmed the slightest bit. "Nobody can know I'm involved. It would jeopardize years of work and thousands of lives. You're on your own for this. When the job is done, a generous, anonymous payment will be made for services rendered."

He left my office, and I followed to make sure he went directly to the elevator. I emerged behind Grayson, and the moment we made it to the lobby, I heard a terrific screech.

Brea launched herself at Cuyler, but Dean caught her around the waist. She dangled from his grasp, her feet not so much kicking as scrambling for traction, and her fingers curved into claws. "You son of a bitch! You have a lot of nerve coming back here. Let me go, Dean."

60

Dean didn't respond or release his hold. Jesse and Frankie moved to create a perimeter in case Cuyler tried something.

Grayson chuckled. "Damn, she's a spitfire. There's nothing more intoxicating than a passionate woman."

"Come closer," Brea said, her green eyes narrow and cold. "I'll show you passion."

"Perhaps another day." Gray lifted a hand in my direction and stepped into the elevator.

Dean released Brea when he saw the doors close. One perfectly sculpted brow rose. "Emergency meeting?"

"Looks that way." I couldn't carry out this assignment alone.

Brea had been scowling at the door, but now she turned to look at me. "I'll make coffee."

She was asking to be included in the meeting. Normally I would have consented, but not this time. "I'd rather you didn't. I want you as far away from this as possible."

"David—"

From the storm in her expression, I knew she was gearing up to remind me that she was part of this team and that I didn't have final say on whether she attended or not. I held up a hand. "I need you to push back a couple of our upcoming jobs. We may need to cancel the ones we have planned for this week. I'd prefer if you started on that."

Shock rendered her speechless, but that only lasted for a few seconds. "You can't be seriously reconsidering. You turned him down."

Dean led the way to the conference room. "Let's get this meeting started. Sugar, you can come, but you can't talk. You don't get to participate in the discussion, and you don't get a vote."

Brea opened her mouth, but Frankie shot her a look that dared her to argue, so she closed it and followed us. In the conference room, she chose a seat next to me and shot me a supportive glance. I guess she knew the stakes were high right now.

I set the two manila file folders on the table. "Carvalho Ferreira Rocha's mainframe is our target. We're to retrieve the most recent memory addition to his server and destroy the rest. Information on Rocha's compound is scant at best because it's in a jungle on the side

Michele Zurlo

of a mountain, so we'll need to do recon before we figure out a strategy. Our deadline is three days from now at midnight, and we'd better not get caught. The US government will disavow any knowledge of us or our activities."

Frankie reached for the top folder. She opened it up. Dean reached for the second one, the one that had incriminating pictures of Brea, and he shuffled through them. Jesse just stared at me. "What's changed since yesterday?"

Dean cleared his throat and passed the file to Jesse. "This."

Jesse perused the photos, and then he nodded.

Frankie didn't bother to look. Her lips curled in disgust. "Blackmail. That bastard."

Her reaction elicited a smile from me, though it may have better resembled a grimace. "That's what I called him."

Brea held her hand out for the file, but Jesse ignored her silent request. So she got up and went to stand behind him, but he closed the cover and set his hand on top of it. She shot me a frustrated scowl, but she didn't say a word. Instead she retreated a few steps and leaned against the wall, her mouth turned down in a pout that I didn't quite buy.

Frankie bit her lip as she looked through the dossier Cuyler had given to me. "Recon can be a two-man job. You and Jesse go. Brea can call our friends at Fournier Security to see if they can take the job you were supposed to go on tomorrow. Dean and I can do our next job, and then we can meet you in San Tesoro when we're finished."

Dean, who'd been looking at the dossier with Frankie, flipped back and forth between two pages. "I'd feel better if Frankie went with you guys. You'll have more use for her kind of firepower than I will." Frankie and Jesse had both been in Delta Force in the Army. Separately they were lethal weapons, but together they were nearly unstoppable. However I was no slouch in that regard.

Jesse gestured to Dean. "Yours is a two-man job. You can't do it with one."

I chimed in next. "I agree. Jesse and I will be fine. We won't engage. We'll just do recon and wait on you two."

Dean tapped through screens on his phone, his mouth pursed. I could almost hear his thoughts as he mentally rearranged schedules. "Let me call Malcolm Legato. He's freelancing for the FBI, and he might be open to doing a job with us."

I'd worked with Malcolm before, and I liked him. He'd left the FBI after they'd brought the hammer down on him for violating protocol one time too many. While he wasn't by any means a loose cannon, I didn't want to go into the unknown with him. "I don't want to bring in someone from the outside for this."

Dean rose, his phone pressed to his ear. "Of course not. Frankie will go with you, and Malcolm will come with me. He can handle a security detail."

Sometimes we had to bend some laws in order to fulfill our missions, and I wasn't sure how Malcolm felt about that. With Brea's life on the line, now was not the time to argue the what ifs. I nodded my consent, and Dean went into the hallway to call Malcolm.

Jesse turned to me, and Brea saw her opportunity. I'd never meant to keep the photos from her, but I understood why Jesse might. She wasn't going to like the fact that her past was being used to blackmail us into action. Jesse wanted to protect her. I did as well, but Brea and I had come to an understanding—though we had a lot of secrets and baggage in the past, we didn't keep anything new or current from each other.

She snagged the file folder, whirling away before Jesse could snatch it back. I admired her graceful reflexes.

Jesse shot me an apologetic frown, and I shrugged in response. "She's going to find out sooner or later. Put them in a safe, and she'll treat it as if you've challenged her to figure out the combination."

Frankie got to her feet and went to Brea. The two of them looked at the pictures together. "Is that Luis Ramirez?" Frankie asked.

"No." I sprang to my feet. "Don't ask her questions about any of those pictures."

At my vehement command, Brea's jaw dropped, and she quickly looked through the remaining pictures. "Why not?"

"Because nothing you say will change the situation."

She closed the folder and handed it to Frankie, and her gaze found me. "You're not going to demand an explanation?"

"No. It's none of my business."

Jesse scooped up the remaining file folder and tugged Frankie toward the door. Frankie thrust the images into Brea's hands before they cleared the room.

The door closed, and she stared at me in silence. "You're not curious? You're not going to ask?"

I was curious as hell, but I wasn't going to ask. "If you feel like you want or need to tell me something, I know you will. Otherwise this stays in the past."

"I don't get it." She tapped the file. "It's just pictures of me with people BS knew."

Could she honestly not know the caliber of person with whom she'd spent her time? She'd once told me that BS consorted with petty criminals, and I believed she thought that was the truth. I threw the file on the table and took her hands in mine. "Those pictures could be used to send you to a black ops prison, the kind where there's no such thing as due process. Evidence, proof, and charges aren't needed to hold you indefinitely."

Her mouth opened and closed, and her eyes grew bright with unshed tears. She swallowed a few times before she found her voice. "He's using me to make you do what he wants, just like last time."

I wasn't following her. "Just like last time?"

"Yeah. He wanted you to stop Brick Dixon, so he used me—he used Chloe Dixon too—to make you take down Dixon." She bit her lip, but she plowed ahead despite her misgivings. "That's the only plausible explanation I can come up with for why he did what he did."

Her conclusions were brilliant, something I hadn't considered at all, but they changed nothing. "Sugar, I have to do this."

The artificial brightness in her eyes betrayed how close she was to spilling tears, but she once again reined in her emotions. "I know."

I put my arms around her, and she melted into my embrace.

"David?" She didn't let go of me, but she did lift her face away from my chest. Her voice was thick with emotion. "Thank you for not asking me to explain the pictures."

I'd come a long way in a few short months. It helped that I'd attended a few therapy session with her and that we'd outlined boundaries and limits with regard to her past. I'd never realized the pain she experienced simply by reliving memories or talking about the past. I kissed her forehead. "I'm here anytime you want to talk, Sugar."

Tears finished pooling and spilled down her cheeks.

I brushed them away with my thumb. "I don't want you to feel guilty about this. When Grayson Cuyler wants something, he finds a way to make it happen. If he hadn't used this avenue, then he would have found another one."

"I'm more pissed than anything else. If he were dangling from a high ledge by the tips of his fingers, I'd pry them loose and wave goodbye."

I laughed, mostly because I couldn't believe she'd actually kill anyone on purpose.

She studied me curiously, unaware of the tears tracking down her face. "Aren't you furious?"

"Yes, but right now I can't afford to give into my anger. I have a job to plan, and you have some schedule shuffling to do for Frankie, Jesse, and me, as well as arrangements to make for Malcolm Legato."

She nodded absently and swiped at the wetness. Her brain had kicked into high gear, and so she'd moved past being pissed. "Okay. I'm on it. Let me tell Jessica that I won't be working in the museum today." I followed her to the door, but she stopped just short of opening it. "There's nothing to stop him from using this against you for the foreseeable future."

There wasn't. Once this job was finished, SAFE Security would focus on finding ways to sever Cuyler's hold over us. For now, I had to get moving to keep the woman I loved from being tossed into a dark prison where the government could conveniently forget about her existence. I know some people dismissed such black sites as fiction, but

I knew for a fact they existed because I'd put people in them. For all I knew, they were still rotting away in anonymity.

Jesse, Frankie, and I threw ourselves into planning for this mission. We combed the reports Grayson had given to us, and we corroborated them by using every available resource. We searched the internet, called in favors, and hacked into secure servers all over the world. Okay, Jesse did all the hacking, but it was a team effort because Frankie and I suggested which countries or agencies might have intel.

Sometime in the afternoon, Brea texted me to be home in time for dinner. Though I could have stayed all night to work on this case, I knew it was best for all of us if we showed up rested and ready tomorrow morning. I also wanted time with Brea before I had to leave again. Sometimes I hated having to leave her so much. She never complained, though. She maintained that she went into this relationship with her eyes wide open. I loved that she didn't nag me about staying home more. That's just not the kind of job I had.

In the elevator of our apartment building, I closed my eyes and worked to shake off the stress and worry of work. The moment I walked through that door, I wanted to be one-hundred percent focused on Brea.

Standing outside the door, I fumbled with my keys. Brea was a fanatic about locking doors. I once tried to play Devil's Advocate by saying that someone who wanted inside wasn't going to let a locked door stand in their way. She'd shot me a level look and replied that we could escape during the noise and effort it would take to kick it in. I'd pointed out that our building didn't have outside fire escapes. The next day, she'd showed me where she'd stowed rappelling equipment so that we could climb down the side of the building.

Before I could insert the correct key, the door opened. Brea stood before me in a deep green mini-dress that brought out her eyes and hid none of her curves. She smiled and stepped back to let me in. "Welcome home, Sir. Dinner will be ready in about fifteen minutes."

Never taking my eyes from her, I closed and locked the door. She'd called me by title, and I wasn't about to overlook the significance of that gesture. I took her in my arms and held her against me. Her soft curves molded to my body, and she slipped her arms around my neck to hold me just as tightly. She offered solace I sorely needed. I buried my face in her neck and inhaled the unique scent of her skin. To me, she smelled like fall—apple cider, sugar donuts, crunching leaves, and the barest hint of snow. I'd never tell her that, though, not after she'd changed her name from Autumn to Brea. Sometimes I was glad that I called her by a nickname instead of her given name because in my head I frequently thought of her as Autumn.

I smoothed my hands down her back until one landed on her ass. As I squeezed gently, I kissed the soft skin of her neck. She let loose a contented sigh and stroked the back of my head. I kissed a path up the column of her throat as I walked her two steps backward until she was caught between my body and the wall. Then I devoured her lips. I took from her because I needed this, and she surrendered everything I sought.

At last I lifted my lips away, and she watched my face, her gaze soft and hazy. "I'm glad you came home."

"So am I." I pushed a lock of hair away from her face, and the love I felt for this woman threatened to cripple me. She was my soul—not just half of it, but the whole fucking thing—and I'd do anything to keep her safe. Right now I wanted to touch her, to take her, to show her how completely she belonged to me. "I want to scene tonight, Sugar."

Her smile matched the softness of her gaze. "It's a good thing I put out a selection of your favorite toys in the bedroom, Sir. I'm also not wearing anything under this dress."

She knew me so well. I chuckled at her thoughtfulness. "Get a condom, and then bend over the table." I eased my weight from her and stepped back to let her carry out the task.

While she was doing that, I changed my clothes and freshened up. The whole time, thoughts of the upcoming mission kept intruding. I pushed them down, but they were always there, hovering on the periphery and threatening to interrupt my night with Sugar.

When I emerged from the bedroom, I found her exactly as I'd ordered, with her legs spread wide and her arms above her head in a position she found comfortable. I had to be careful with her left shoulder due to a car accident she'd been in several years ago. She'd embellished a bit by putting a towel on the table to cushion where the edge would dig into her thighs. She'd also taken it upon herself to get the lube. Though she couldn't see it because her face was turned toward the kitchen, I smiled at her thoughtfulness.

She didn't move when I lifted the skirt of her dress to expose her sweet ass. I traced my fingertips lightly over her flesh, and a small, contented sigh escaped her mouth. "Do you like that, Sugar?"

"I love when you touch me, Sir."

I widened the area of my foray, trailing that touch she loved down her thighs and between her legs. I stroked her labia ever so gently. "You're not going to climax before dinner, but I promise that by the time you pass out tonight, you'll have had more than you wanted."

"As long as I please you, Sir, then I'm happy."

I unzipped my jeans and stared at her luscious ass while stroking myself. When I was good and hard, I rolled the condom on and coated it with lube. Then I drizzled it along her crack and massaged it into her anus. She exhaled when I penetrated that tight muscle with one finger, and she moaned when I inserted a second finger. I loved taking her this way.

Lining my cockhead up with her sphincter, I pushed lightly to test the give. "Exhale, Sugar. I'm not going to be gentle."

"Ready when you are, Sir."

She breathed out, and I surged forward, burying myself completely in one thrust. I glanced at her hands to make sure she wasn't making a safeword gesture where she crossed the first two fingers on either hand. Her palms were flat against the table, and she'd lifted her ass to meet my thrust, so I wasted no time. She felt so damn good—hot and tight and completely mine. I fucked her fast and hard, pounding her like veal. As I approached frenzy, I grabbed a handful of her hair and pulled her head back, forcing her to bow off the table.

She cried out, surprised more than anything else, and adjusted her arms to better support her torso.

"You're mine, Sugar."

"Completely, Sir."

The fire in my balls detonated. I surged forward, burying myself as far as I could go, and let my climax wash over me.

Brea: My Submissive Side

Abruptly he released his hold on my hair, and I caught myself before I took a header into the table. His grip on my hip hadn't eased, so I didn't move. I waited for him to recover. His cock pulsed inside me, reminding me that our bodies were joined and that I belonged to him. Though I hadn't climaxed, I felt more satisfied and complete than if I had. Right now he was floating on a sea of post-coital bliss, and I had given that to him.

I'd given myself to my Sir.

Submission was so much sweeter now that he wasn't demanding it all the time. I'd found that I needed this. I needed our scenes, and I needed to serve him—but I didn't need it 24/7. Our relationship had grown a lot in the past few months, and I felt closer to David than I ever had before.

His softened cock slid out of me, and I heard David's footsteps heading toward the bathroom. Mostly likely he was going to dispose of the condom. Normally I'd stay where I was, but the oven timer went off, and I needed to get dinner before it burned.

When David returned, he found me in the kitchen, putting the finishing touches on dinner. He pressed a kiss to my neck. "I used a ton of lube, Sugar. Why don't you go clean up, and I'll finish here."

"Thank you, Sir. Would you like me to sit at the table or at your feet?"

He thought for a moment, his hand splayed over his shirt and his thumb absently tapping on his sternum. "You're going to sit on my lap, and I'm going to feed you."

We ate a leisurely dinner. I sat on his lap, and we snuggled, munched, and talked about everything and nothing. We avoided the elephant in the room and pretended this was just a regular, intimate evening.

Soon our plate—he'd piled it high for both of us—was empty. He nuzzled my neck. "Sugar, tomorrow I want you to set a date for our wedding."

That's the last thing I had expected him to say. My jaw dropped. "Sir, that's something we should do together."

He inhaled, and I knew he was losing himself in my scent. Then his grip on my hip tightened. "I know, but things are happening so fast. You have access to the schedule. Find a time when everyone isn't booked, and black out the date."

There was more to scheduling a wedding than that. I needed to find a venue and someone to officiate. I stroked his hair. "Do you have an opinion on where you want this to happen or who you want to conduct the ceremony?"

"Nope." He lifted his head and fixed me with a dorky grin. "But Dean is a registered reverend. He's conducted several ceremonies for friends in the lifestyle. If you're okay with having him officiate, then that's an easy one."

That sounded great to me. "So you'll be okay with any venue I pick?"

He traced his fingertips along my cheek. "As long as I get to marry you, I don't care where it happens."

With that, he captured my lips in a searing kiss, and I knew the direction of his thoughts had shifted. He lifted me, and by the time the kiss ended, I found myself seated on the edge of our bed. Sir lifted my dress over my head, baring my body to his heated gaze. He stepped back and looked at me, caressing me with just the power of his eyes. I remained still, absorbing this silent dominance that fed my submission.

Under his open admiration, I felt beautiful, cherished, and loved. Spoken words were unnecessary because his gaze said enough for ten sonnets. My nipples pebbled in anticipation, and my pussy had been weeping for a while.

David lost his shirt, tossing it onto the back of a chair next to the table where I'd set up a selection of his favorite toys. He had a magnificent chest—corded muscles topped with broad shoulders. A small trail of blond hair began just below his sternum and continued into his jeans. He let me look for a few seconds before he turned away to peruse his choices.

When I set up for a scene where I didn't know what he'd planned, I always put out a selection of impact implements—floggers, a crop, and two canes—and I set out his favorite dildos, vibrators, and butt plugs. In addition to the usual, I'd included a spatula, a wooden spoon, and a set of nipple clamps.

He picked up the black, molded plastic spatula, studied it thoughtfully, and then he cast a crafty smile over his shoulder at me. "You want me to scramble your eggs, Sugar?"

It wasn't what I'd expected him to say. That, combined with the nervous energy that built whenever we began a scene, made me giggle. "If you want, Sir."

He came closer and motioned to the foot of the bed with the spatula. "I want you to lay on your back, pussy positioned at the edge, and hold your knees out of the way."

I knew the exact pose he described, and so I rolled to the foot of the bed, lifted my knees, and held them with a hand on each shin. Sir looked me over, his gaze turning hard and possessive, thoroughly dominant. Though I was spread wide open, heat poured from between my legs.

He smacked the spatula against the tender flesh of the inside of his forearm. Then he did it several times more, each time harder than the last. A frown tugged at the corners of his mouth. "It doesn't pack much force."

"No, it doesn't, Sir." A spatula would be a fun warm-up, but it would never actually hurt or get me to subspace.

He peppered my ass and thighs with a series of slaps. "Did you put this out because you want to use it on me?"

"Interesting idea, Sir, but you're the Dom in this scene." Maybe I'd been reading up on pervertibles with the hope that he'd eventually let me try out some impact play on him. I knew he'd like it.

The next few slaps circled the outside of my labia. It was a very light, thuddy feeling, but the sensations barely registered. Even when the blows struck my pink parts or landed directly on my clit, they weren't all that noticeable. If anything, it might drive me insane by denying my need for something with more bite.

He continued the slaps, traveling up my stomach to my breasts. My pebbled nipples registered a little more sensation. I closed my eyes to focus the feeling, and he stopped. He set the spatula down with the flat end between my breasts, and he went back to the table.

"I'm not a fan of the wooden spoon," he said. "These break too easily." He returned with four black cuffs, two of which he buckled around my wrists. The others went around my ankles. Sir used latches and chains to attach the ones on my ankles to eye hooks screwed into the ceiling rafters. Now my legs were bound high in the air and spread wide open.

With my arms, he was a little more inventive. He threaded a metal rod through a pool noodle, which he passed under my neck before securing my arms out to each side. This position didn't aggravate the shoulder injury I'd sustained from a car accident years ago, and it provided great support for my neck, which somehow kept my lower back from hurting as well.

"How does it feel, Sugar?" He ran his hands over my skin, starting at my wrists and not stopping until he reached my feet.

I wiggled my fingers and toes. "Exquisite, Sir."

He chuckled at my hyperbole, but I could tell he appreciated the sentiment. He leaned over and planted a kiss on my lips. His bare chest tickled against my breasts. "I love you, Sugar."

"I love you too, Sir."

"I'm not going to go easy on you tonight."

"I hope not, Sir."

He pressed red foam balls into each of my palms, and then he held a ball gag in front of my lips. Automatically I opened. Not only did he like the way I looked in a gag, but I tended to get very loud during scenes, and the neighbors had registered a few complaints with the building's residential board members. We'd received six "official notices" to keep the screaming to a minimum. Of course, David was also loud during sex, but he never wore a gag.

There was something about being tied up and gagged, completely at David's mercy, that brought peace to my core the way nothing else quite could. I knew he was about to torture me, to strip every ounce of control away while he used my body to feed his sadistic needs. Yes, I was nervous, but in a good way because I trusted him more than I'd trusted anyone in my life except Jessica.

He stopped again to look at me, but only for a second. A hard mask slipped over his features. Though his brown eyes had darkened, they glimmered with satisfaction.

The flogging came first. Deerskin massaged my ass and thighs. I felt myself falling deeper into submission as he warmed up my skin. Even when his expert aim found my breasts, I didn't arch or protest. The spatula he'd set on my chest didn't move.

When he felt I was prepared enough, he plunged several fingers inside my pussy. With unerring precision, he found my sweet spot and worked my clit with his thumb. I tossed my head, but the pool noodle kept it from moving too far, and I moaned behind the gag.

Pleasure bloomed, spreading in all directions, and he withdrew his fingers. They glistened with my juices, and he licked them clean. "You taste so fucking sweet, Sugar." With that, he swiped his tongue once from hole to clit. Then he crossed the room, grabbed a few things from the table, and returned to me.

The nipple clamps I'd put out were the kind that tightened down without covering the nipple. He screwed the first one on my pebbled nipple, tightening it mercilessly even after I cried out. Tears pricked my eyes, and he only smiled as he affixed the other clamp just as viciously. Then he picked up the spatula again and brought it down sharply on my clamped nipple. The kitchen implement I'd considered harmless had transformed. A million shards of pain radiated through my breasts and down my arms. I cried out, but the gag muffled the sound.

Back and forth, he drummed on my poor, overly sensitized breasts. The unrelenting pain had my eyes rolling back into my head. Wetness tracked across my temples and into my hair. After a time, he stopped, and I held my breath.

"Exhale, Sugar, or this is going to hurt even more." He loosened the clamps quickly, and the returning blood flow sent pinpricks everywhere. I squeezed the foam balls in my palms and breathed through the dissipating pain.

As I recovered, I felt his fingers at my back entrance, smearing lube. I closed my eyes and exhaled as he passed a string of anal beads, each one successively larger, through my tight opening. Next he inserted a pink silicone dildo into my pussy. It was shaped like a dick, complete with a thicker head and veins on the shaft. He fucked me with it while working the anal beads in and out of my ass. Pleasure built in my core, and I rotated my hips to meet each thrust. My moans sounded deep in my throat, barely quieted by the gag, and soon my climax broke.

David, my Sir, knew exactly when I came, but he didn't stop fucking me with that dildo or rhythmically sliding the beads through my sphincter. It wasn't long before a second orgasm, this one larger, took me.

This time he stopped. As he extracted the dildo and anal beads, I struggled to heave breaths through my nose. My chest rose and fell rapidly, and I knew he was just getting started. Sir loved nothing more than to torture me by forcing me to orgasm.

Next he brought a vibrator. He turned it on the pulse setting and held it against my clit. It was too much too soon, and my clit retreated. "What a naughty, bratty little nub. A little punishment should encourage it to behave."

He slathered the vibrator with lube, and then he worked it into my pussy, thrusting it in and pulling it out—only to thrust it deeper the next time. When it was completely in, he turned up the pulse setting so that it buzzed twice and then rested for a heartbeat.

Instead of watching, he pinched my clit hard, forcing the tip to peak out. Then he flicked his tongue over it. Electric shocks, cold and so very hot, radiated to the soles of my feet. I lifted off the bed and banged my mons into his face. He pushed me back down, and the next thing I knew he had the crop in hand. He lifted it high and brought it down across the back of my left thigh. It stung, and more tears leaked from my eyes. He did it twice more.

"Stay still, Sugar. I get to taste the sweet treats that belong to me." He bent down again, and he sealed his lips around my clit and sucked hard. The crop in his hand rested against my tenderized thigh, reminding me to use all my willpower to avoid moving.

It felt good and it hurt. As he sucked my clit into his mouth, extending it almost to my breaking point, his hands roamed my flesh. His possessive touch quieted my resistance and soothed my nerves. Soon only the pleasure of serving him mattered. The pain melted away, and a small climax flooded my system with pleasure.

He turned up the setting on the vibrator, and the serotonin fled my system. I don't know how long it took, but the next orgasm robbed me of reason. I thrashed madly, a creature of overripe passion driven to the brink. Dimly I was aware of Sir turning off the vibrator and pulling it from my pussy.

I panted through the gag, gasping for oxygen. Sir unbuckled the strap holding it in place and eased it from between my lips. I gulped air.

"What's your color, Sugar?" He hovered over me, concern lighting his dark eyes.

"Green, Sir." I knew he wasn't ready to call it a night and just fuck me the old-fashioned way.

"Great. Don't forget your secondary signal." He held the gag to my lips. "I'd prefer to leave you ungagged, Sugar. I love hearing you moan, scream, and beg." He'd put in an offer on our closest neighbor's condo, but she was still mulling it over.

I responded to the yearning in his tone. "Sir, maybe if you didn't, she'd get tired of the noise and finally sell the unit."

"You're such a brat." He tossed the gag aside. "I like the way you think. Okay. Don't hold back."

The next toy he selected had an impossibly huge circumference. I hated and loved that thing. It stretched me to the limit, and it never failed to produce a huge, earth-shattering orgasm. Fear seized me, and I shook my head. "Please, Sir. Not that."

"Yes, Sugar. This."

"I'm begging you, Sir." With my tone, my eyes, and my body language.

"I appreciate that, Sugar." The whole time, he pumped his lubed hand up and down the shaft of that thing. The end of it tapered, not even pretending it needed a ridge or a head to get the job done. Then he pressed it to my opening and slowly inserted it.

My pussy wept as it expanded to accommodate this eggplant wanna-be. My wetness combined with the lubrication to make it glide right in. Every fold inside my vagina was stretched to the max, every delicate nerve exposed. There was no hunting for my sweet spot because every nanometer of my pussy was in intimate contact with the dildo. He slid it in and out slowly, fucking me gently.

It didn't matter. My eyes watered and my very being lengthened. In minutes, my pussy contracted, squeezing that unyielding thing so hard it hurt. Icy waves of my climax pelted me with shards of pleasure and pain. It was too much. It was always too much.

"Please, Sir."

He chuckled, his evil laugh compounding the helplessness I felt. "Another one, Sugar?"

"No. Please, no." I shook my head vehemently, probably bruising my shoulder through the pool noodle.

"Yes. Ask for it."

There was no way in hell I was asking for another orgasm. I'd had enough. My pussy was tired, and the pleasure of climax had transformed into a kind of torture. "No. I don't want anymore. Please, Sir, let me give you a blowjob, or maybe you want to fuck my ass again?"

Something whistled through the air, and a sharp line of pain stung my ass cheek. Sir held the thin rattan cane in his hand and regarded me grimly. "Ask for another orgasm, Sugar. Beg for it."

I shook my head, and he swung again, this time laying a stripe on the other cheek. Even with all the feel-good chemicals traveling through my veins thanks to the orgasms, the cane wasn't something I could hold out against for very long, and he knew it.

Two more stripes, and I thrashed my head in denial. A third, and I bent my knees, lifting my ass into the air. This made me acutely aware that he hadn't removed the large dildo from my pussy. He waited until I'd settled my ass back down to deliver another blow from the cane.

I broke. Tears streamed from my eyes, and I hiccupped. "Please may I have another orgasm?"

"Certainly." He slid the huge dildo out, drizzled more lube over it, and put it back inside me.

It didn't take long for me to realize that he's used spicy lube this time. As it penetrated my tissues, my pussy heated. "Sir," I whimpered.

"Perfect," he said. "Surrender to me, my lovely sub."

I already had, body and soul, and so I gave myself over to his needs once again. I don't know how long it took for him to coax me to orgasm, but by the time it throbbed through me on unwelcome waves, I was too spent to sob, beg, protest, or resist.

He untied my legs first, and then he helped me to sit up. He eyeballed the red foam balls clutched in each of my hands before he slid me to the floor and positioned me on my knees. I faced him, my arms still bound to the metal pole wrapped with a foam sheath, and bowed my head. Juices dripped from my pussy and smeared all over my thighs. My face was a mess from crying and drooling, and my hair was matted.

He stroked my hair back from my face. "You are so fucking beautiful, Sugar. I'm going to memorize this moment, and when I'm missing you so badly it hurts, I'm going to see you here, kneeling before me, and I'll know everything is going to be fine."

Deep in the throes of submission and hovering on the edge of subspace, I responded to the awe in his tone. I lifted my gaze to see his rock hard erection staring me in the face. As he lowered his jeans, I opened my mouth. I wished I had my hands free to hold and fondle him, but I didn't, and so I made do with my lips, teeth, and tongue. He thrust into the only orifice I had left that didn't ache, taking me with careful jabs. He moaned and grunted, increasing his pace and the volume of his pleasure. Before long, he thrust to the back of my throat, and his hot semen spurted into me.

I collapsed forward, out of energy and enough will to remain upright. Vaguely I was aware of him untying my arms and lifting me. He wrapped me in a soft blanket and held me against his chest. "Thank you, Sugar. You were very good tonight. You pleased me greatly." He stroked my hair and pressed kisses to my forehead as he murmured sentiments of praise and love.

Much later, I awoke to the feel of his hands moving over my stomach and caressing my hips. I was in our bed, and the lights were off. My face and body had been cleaned, and my hair was no longer matted.

I rolled toward him and flopped a hand onto his shoulder. "Sir?"

"I have to leave soon, Sugar." He pulled me closer, so that my body was pressed against his, and he captured my lips in a slow kiss.

As much as I didn't want him to go, I knew better than to ask. The only outcome would be that he would feel guilty rather than focusing on his mission. And so I yielded to his kiss and let my hands roam his sleep-warmed skin. Soon his kiss grew more urgent, and he rolled us so that he was on top. I spread my legs to urge him closer, but he took his time. He touched me everywhere, reverent caresses that said without words how much he loved me, and I proclaimed my love for him the same way.

Before long he slipped his cock into my still-sensitive pussy, and he made love to me. We came together, trembling in each other's arms, and he held me for precious minutes afterward.

A shiver of revulsion ran through me as I thought about what a horrible person that man had turned out to be. The first time I'd noticed Grayson Cuyler, I'd thought he was handsome and that maybe he was interested in Jessica. It had been all downhill after that. Even finding out that he was an undercover NEO spy didn't excuse his behavior. Kidnapping, and now blackmail. Sheesh. I wouldn't put it past him to be playing multiple sides. These kinds of cons were addictive, as

I knew from not only watching BS perpetrate them, but from participating in them myself.

Having the upper hand among dangerous individuals was a rush. Wielding power like that—nothing compared to it, not even being a Domina. Everything I did in that capacity was safe, sane, and consensual. Nothing about pulling a con fell within those parameters. A con was all about taking advantage of a person or situation; the grifter always tried to benefit at another's expense. Grayson Cuyler was a dangerous man because he also believed he was doing the right thing.

I took my time showering, and I lingered over breakfast in our empty apartment. Sometimes when David left, it took me a few hours to find my bearings and remember how to operate without him around. I was staring out the window at the bleak wintry day when a knock at the door startled me back into the present.

Jessica frequently came over when she knew I was alone. Sometimes she brought Sylvia or Warren with her, and once she'd brought Leon, our little brother who I still didn't know very well. Even though we'd arm wrestled and I'd baked cupcakes for him, he and I had not advanced past the awkward conversation phase of our relationship. Nikki Eliachevsky, my shrink, said it would take time. I didn't know how much time it was supposed to take, but I was beginning to think that we were locked into a behavior pattern that would never change.

On the other side of the door, I found Mrs. Lashell, her pinched features and scowl lines not as deep today. She handed me a paper. "Eviction proceedings will begin next week."

Scanning the missive, I realized it was a notice that we'd violated the building noise ordinance one time too many, and now they were going to try to force us to sell. I handed it back. "Good luck. My fiancé is wealthy, and I'm stubborn." Nothing would induce me to move now, not with this woman trying to take my first real home from me.

She handed me another sheaf of papers. "Or you can accept this counteroffer."

I scanned the bold print, and I realized the counteroffer asked for twice the value of the property. David had offered a more than fair price last month. This was robbery. No—this was blackmail. Fury, hot and sweet, burned in my belly. I shoved all the papers at her, jabbing at her midsection to force her to take them. "No fucking way."

Her mouth set hard, and those scowl lines deepened. I had no idea how old she was, but I estimated mid-forties. Constant disapproval had taken its toll on her face, and now she looked sour all the time. "Then you'll be evicted. Either way, I win."

Channeling my inner Domina, I took one step forward. I was perhaps an inch or so taller, and I used that to my advantage. She took a step back, then another and another. When she stopped running from me, I parked my hands on my hips and purred a promise. "You have no idea how badly you're going to lose."

She clenched a fist. "You can't threaten me."

I smiled slowly, a leopard about to have a tasty meal. "That's not a threat, Mrs. Lashell. That's a promise." I let that last part linger for a moment, relishing the exact moment she realized she'd chosen to tangle with the wrong person. Then I went back inside. Ten minutes ago, I'd been prepared to wallow in depression all day, but now I was invigorated—and motivated. David's mission wasn't going to be a success, but I bet I could still save the day.

Jessica was in our shop when I got there. Paste smudged her cheek, and stray curls dangled over her eyes. She grinned as I came inside. "I was wondering if you'd show up or if I'd have to drag you off the couch."

"Unexpected Treasures." I'd been thinking of names for our museum and shop. Right now, we had more items for sale than treasure to display. "And I want to show you the legends of treasure I've been researching. A couple of these look like they have a good chance of actually existing."

"I've been reading through your notes." She gestured toward her work table. The trunk Jesse had brought yesterday was now completely bare of all decoration, revealing a wood-and-metal construction over a plain surface. "I found something interesting here that I want to show you first."

Looking closer, I wondered what mystery she'd found inside a random trunk. "You didn't say if you liked my idea for the shop."

"It's not terribly specific."

"That's a good thing. We can stock unique items. It'll keep customers coming back, and it'll allow us to pretty much sell anything we want. And the museum side will fit in with your furniture and art parts." A few months ago, when I'd decided to devote my time to treasure hunting, I had turned down David's offer to work for SAFE Security. Since then, I'd bowed to Jesse, Frankie, and Dean's repeated entreaties that they couldn't live without my managerial skills. I'd been taking care of them and not contributing much to our shop, and I aimed to change that now.

She nodded. "Okay. Let's go with that. Unexpected Treasures. I like it." She slid a thin, leatherbound volume toward me. "You have to see this, Brea. It's amazing."

It looked old. The leather was cracked and faded, and the papers inside were as well. The first page, a thin vellum sheet, proclaimed: *Diary of Poncia Dominguez Baeza, Barcelona, Spain 1593*. The loopy letters and flourishes made it difficult to read. The next page had a date of *27 Septiembre*.

The diary wasn't thick. It contained seventeen pages. Some may have been lost to time, as many of the pages left were torn or portions of them had crumbled away. From what I could gather, it was the account of a group of five Spanish explorers, including Baeza, who had found gold in the mountains of Central America. They'd enslaved some of the local indigenous peoples and forced them to work in the mine for four years. They abused and mistreated the slaves, subjecting them to starvation, regular beatings, and subhuman living conditions. I hated this man more with every word I read. During this time, they'd reaped the rewards of their endeavor, paying Spain their due and coming away with unimaginable riches.

Their run ended abruptly when the main shaft collapsed, trapping or killing all of the slaves and three of Baeza's four partners. Then the account, already full of horrible deeds, got weird. Baeza swears the natives put a curse on him and Rico, the only name he used to refer to the other surviving partner. He writes of trying to dig out the shaft, only to hear demonic whispers of his doom.

Under the thumb of the equally greedy Spanish monarchy, he and Rico tried to enslave more locals. However this time, "the spirits of those wronged rose up to do murder to Rico. His body lifted on demonic currents and was torn asunder."

I glanced up to see Jessica watching me read, an expectant expression on her face. "How did the diary come to be here?"

Her eyes lit, and she gestured to the trunk. "It was hidden in the lining of the trunk. I found moth-eaten silk under the decoupage, and when I removed it, the diary fell out."

"Wasn't Baeza killed by the spirits too?"

She shrugged. "It's not a complete account, but there are several maps at the end, where he warns people to stay away. It's in line with the research you're doing on that Spanish mine legend."

I set the missive down. The maps, when laid over a modern one, would indicate that the treasure was in San Tesoro, not far from where David, Jesse, and Frankie were probably standing right now. The legend I'd been researching indicated gold in a collapsed mine shaft in Colorado. "Jessica, I appreciate what you've done, but—"

"What I've done?" She came closer, and that's when I noticed she was using a cane. It was about freaking time. Her PT kept admonishing her for not using one. She leaned it against the table and put her hands on my shoulders. "Brea, we have to go look for this treasure. It says there's a mother lode of gold in there, stacked and waiting for us."

Though I wasn't feeling at all happy or optimistic, I smiled at her thoughtfulness. "Jessica, this isn't your best work. First, he would have written it in Spanish, not English."

While I could read and write a little in Spanish, Jessica had only learned to speak it. She sighed and dropped her hands. "But we wouldn't realize that, right? We'd just pick up and go."

She was looking for excuses to get us down there, and a cover story once we were there. I loved her for it. "I was just going to go down there and knock on Charlie's door."

Jessica snorted. "He's not going to give you the server."

"No, but I spent some time researching the area when I thought they might take the approach you and I recommended."

"Idiots." Jessica scowled, but hers was cute and reminded me of when we were kids. "Our plan had a much higher chance of success."

I agreed with Jessica, but I knew why David had rejected the plan. It put Frankie in a very vulnerable position, and the trio was more familiar with smash-and-grab than with infiltration. That kind of con was where Jessica and I felt comfortable. "There's a car show opening Wednesday. They're setting up today and tomorrow, and the big donors are allowed private showings tonight and tomorrow night."

Her eyes lit. "Charlie always said he liked fast women and even faster cars."

"He's going to be there. It'll look more natural if we run into him in the vicinity." I gestured to the diary. "And we can bring this. Charlie will buy it as our reason for being in San Tesoro."

Jessica perched on the stool I'd just vacated. "You need to book us flights, and then we need to pack. I'm trying to remember the names we used when we knew Charlie?"

I remembered them very well. "Ara and Isa, the Bella sisters. You hated them. You and BS got into a huge fight about it because you didn't want to be called Isabella." I hadn't cared. Names came and went, and we rarely were allowed to choose our own. "Let me book the flights. If I remember correctly, there's one out of here in four hours. That'll put us in San Tesoro by midnight."

This timeline would give us less than forty-eight hours to get into Charlie's compound and steal the server. Thanks to Jesse, at least I now knew what one looked like.

David: Another Day at the Office

I threw my bag on the foot of one of the double beds in the one hotel room Brea had booked for us in Cadez, the village nearest the reported location of Rocha's compound. "Should we talk about the elephant in the room?"

Frankie claimed the other bed. She tossed her sleek ponytail over one shoulder, opened her luggage, and began inventorying the state of her equipment. "You mean the fact that we have a 70% chance of failing?"

Jesse continued his sweep for bugs of the listening or recording variety. "That gives us a 30% chance of success. If we can buy this hotel, then we'll be able to expand our travel packages to include this Central American gem."

I knew that Jesse's response had been calibrated to follow our cover story—that of executives from a travel company looking to expand the range of offerings to our exclusive member hotels. However that's not the kettle of worms I'd meant to open.

Frankie disassembled and reassembled her sidearm, the parts clicking and sliding easily in her knowledgeable grasp. "I don't trust the scant intel available online. This is a long-term deal, one where we visit regularly so that we can understand the lay of the land, the seasonal weather patterns, and how tourism is supported by the local government."

I agreed that Cuyler hadn't given us nearly enough. We all knew we'd been fed the bare minimum. There was a better than even chance that the military had already tried to get inside Rocha's compound. It made me doubt the chances of success for our surgical strike, especially because Frankie was right—we needed months to study the situation. We needed to know Rocha's schedule and habits, as well as those of his men. And there was no way a criminal of his caliber had survived this long down here without having ties to key players in local or regional government and military.

Jesse flipped a switch on his scanner and set it on the table that held a TV. "It's clean. I'm setting it to jam signals in case someone should decide to suddenly start listening in." He rolled his shoulders and turned to me. "I'm surprised you'd lead off with a question about the mission."

"I didn't." I glanced at Frankie who was feeling around in the bottom of her bag for something. "I meant to ask when we were going to meet Frankie's new boyfriend."

She threw a forbidding frown at me before returning to her task. "Never."

Jesse stretched out on the other side of Frankie's bed. He laced his fingers behind his head and turned his full attention to her. "Why not?"

"My private life is none of your beeswax." She lifted a travel toiletry sack from her bag. Jesse snatched it away, and she glared at him, a threat of violence implicit in her unspoken warning.

"Since when?" I moved to block her path to the bathroom.

She whirled, her black eyes glittering with yellow caution signs. "Since the last time you poked your fucking noses in my business."

Confused, I stared mutely. It had been years since she'd brought a boyfriend around, which is probably why I'd forgotten that she had a personal life. Maybe we hadn't thought he was good enough for her, but we'd all been friendly. Two days ago when she'd shown up to our emergency meeting wearing an evening gown, I'd been surprised, but I'd been too worried about Cuyler and focused on business to ask Frankie anything.

She rolled her eyes and shoved to push me aside. Though I knew I gambled with my physical well-being, I stood my ground.

Before she could slam me in some painful way, I held up a hand. "Frankie, if you didn't like the way we behaved, you can just tell us. I didn't think we chased off the last guy. We were nice to him."

She stared for the space of three heartbeats. "He wasn't the last one, dumbass. I've had three serious relationships since then. Unlike you, I don't bring them to work to fuck in my office." She shot her withering glare in Jesse's direction. "Or the hallway outside the gym."

Jesse sat up. "You saw that?"

Her spine and shoulders remained ramrod straight, a perfect, military T. "The whole place is on camera. Dean and I wanted to make sure there wasn't another problem in the building. You two were hard to miss."

"Huh. Good plan." He rubbed his stubbly scalp. "I should have thought of that."

"When was this? What the hell happened?" I wasn't following. "Who did you have sex with?"

Suddenly he wouldn't meet my gaze. "Um, last night Jessica set off an alarm because she went out the third floor window to the fire escape. I talked her out of having a cigarette."

She wasn't my sister, but besides me, she was the most important person in Brea's world—so she mattered deeply to me. I didn't keep the sarcasm from my tone. "And one thing led to another? So naturally you had sex with her."

The sheepish light vanished from Jesse's pale eyes. His lips thinned. "We're not talking about me and Jessica. We were talking about the fact that Frankie doesn't want to be friends with us anymore."

Put in such stark terms, I realized that Jesse was right. Friends shared their lives with each other, and somewhere along the line, Frankie had stopped. And we hadn't noticed. I crossed my arms over my chest, mostly because I felt like an ass, and I moved out of Frankie's way. "Frankie, I'd give my life for you."

She exhaled a growl. "And I'd do the same for either of you fools." She looked from Jesse to me and back again. "We're still friends. I just want clear lines between my personal and professional lives."

None of the rest of us had gone through any length to keep our private lives away from our professional ones. Whenever Jesse, Dean, or I had a girlfriend, we socialized them with the group. I didn't see how keeping everybody separate could lead to a lasting relationship.

I pointed out the most obvious incongruity. "But you don't mind socializing with Brea or Jessica. You're friendly and welcoming. Brea thinks you're her friend."

Jesse bounced up and boxed Frankie in from the other direction. "And you gave Jessica the cane I had specially made for you after you broke your ankle in Syria."

The cane hid a stiletto blade in the shaft, but it was cleverly made so that airport security scanners would think it had a metal core, which was easily explained away as a stability feature. She'd loved the gift, and she'd used it on several missions.

Frankie snatched her toiletry bag from Jesse. "You drama queens are making a huge deal out of nothing." With that, she disappeared into the bathroom.

I faced Jesse. "How did we not notice this?"

"We're jackasses, and we figured she just hadn't met anybody worth mentioning. Real friends would have asked."

This was getting all kinds of touchy-feely, and we were leaving my comfort zone. I half wished I'd lied and kept the conversation on the viability of our mission. With an aggravated sigh, I went back to my bag to double check its contents. "I feel like I did ask. I distinctly remember asking regularly how things were going." Searching my memory banks, I could vividly picture sitting in Frankie's office after she'd been gone for a few days, asking how she'd spent the time. Her responses had always been detailed enough to avoid questions, and I realized they'd also been vague.

In the meantime, I had to deal with something else Frankie had said. With a reluctant breath, I faced Jesse. "You slept with Jessica?"

"I did."

While Jesse had lived the life of a Casanova, I didn't think he'd fool around with Jessica. "When's the wedding?" I may have skipped a few steps, but I didn't want Jesse to think I was okay with them having a casual relationship.

His chuckle had a defeated edge. "I'm having enough trouble convincing her to let me take her out to dinner. She, um, she has some issues with men and relationships."

I lifted a brow. "She might object to your lengthy past."

"Nope. Her past is just as lengthy, and she wasn't as kind to her exes." He stared out the lone window at the whitewashed stucco wall of the next building. "Brea came to see me about this already, only she seems to think I'm the one in danger. Maybe she's right. I haven't felt this way about a woman since Josie died, and Jessica is fighting against me with everything she's got."

Jesse rarely mentioned the brief marriage to his high school sweetheart that began shortly after graduating from high school and ended tragically in a car accident three years later. He had been deployed overseas while his young wife had been working and attending community college. Josie had languished in the hospital for thirty-six hours before she perished from her injuries. Jesse had been en route when he received the news. He'd never quite forgiven himself for not being there with her at the end.

Satisfied that his intentions were good, I let it go.

While Jesse and I both beat ourselves up, the toilet flushed, and water ran. Frankie emerged. She looked at Jesse, and then her hawkish gaze landed on me. "Oh, for Pete's sake. You're pouting?"

"We're not pouting." Jesse's denial sounded kind of petulant.

"I was just thinking about how it would suck to lose your friendship." I zipped my bag and tossed it into a corner.

"You're not losing my friendship." She closed her eyes, and her lips moved as she counted ten. "Look, it's not easy being the only female at SAFE Security."

From his perch on the edge of the bed we'd share tonight, Jesse frowned. "We've taken great pains to not treat you differently."

"Yes, and I appreciate that. But outside of the job—" She broke off and shook her head. "I liked it better when you were oblivious."

I settled into the lone chair in the room and armed myself to hear something I might not like. Thankfully my association with Brea had taught me to gird my loins and take it like a man. "I'd like you to continue. Outside the job—what?"

Frankie crossed her arms, a defensive move that seemed foreign on someone who had always been so welcoming and friendly. She faced Jesse. "Three summers ago, you took me with you to Florida one weekend to visit your mom. A bunch of your aunts, uncles, and cousins were there for some kind of impromptu family reunion."

Jesse nodded and smiled fondly. "I remember."

"You went off with the men to handle the outdoor cooking and beer drinking, while I got stuck in the kitchen with the women."

"You didn't have to stay there."

Her snort of disgust put us both in our places, and I hadn't even said anything. "Yes, I did. I'm a woman, so I'm expected to do what the women do. When I was in Afghanistan, it was my job to talk to the women in the villages." She faced me next. "And you expect me to be friends with your fiancée and her sister."

Brea would be crushed if she found out that Frankie didn't really want to be her friend. There were very few people with whom Brea felt comfortable enough to open up, and Frankie was one of them. I sat up straighter. "If you don't want to be friends with Brea, you don't have to. I thought you liked her."

"I do. She's a fighter, and she doesn't pull her punches. Figuratively. Literally, she's still got work to do. Right now I think she's more invested in having a friendship with me than you are. But consider this, David: Let's say I do bring around a boyfriend. I introduce him to the three of you. Let's say he isn't immediately intimidated by the alpha, macho, bullshit you three like to throw around. Then what? He hangs with you guys, and next thing you know, he's your friend and I'm not."

I exchanged a look with Jesse, silently conversing about how we'd treated Frankie's last known boyfriend. He'd been a lawyer, a high-powered type who drove a Jaguar and liked to ski in Switzerland. He'd liked to brag about his expensive watch and his collection of hand-crafted swords. We weren't against those things, but we failed to see where he had much in common with Frankie—other than the fact that he'd been half Indian. We'd taken him to a monster truck rally, where he'd drank too much and told us that Frankie was an acrobat in the sack. He'd spent the rest of the night puking, and a few weeks later, he broke up with Frankie because she wasn't a vegetarian.

"You're upset because we tried to be friends with your boyfriend, and you're upset that we want you to be friends with our girlfriends?" I had to clarify. "Because that sounds a little sexist, Frankie. Brea is friends with Jesse and Dean too. She went to see Phantom of the Opera with Dean two weeks ago. And we invited you to that monster truck rally. You said you didn't want to go. You said a little male bonding would be good for him."

She stared out the window at the side of the building next to us. "He was jealous of my friendship with you guys. Since I've stopped commingling my personal and professional lives, I haven't had to deal with petty jealousies."

"Sounds like you're dating the wrong guys." I came back quickly because there was no way in hell I was going to let her out of this one. "Brea wasn't sure about you at first, but once she got to know you, she realized that you're just one of the guys." I gestured at the sleeping arrangements. "She didn't blink at booking just one room for the three of us."

"Well," Jesse rubbed his hand over his head, a sign that he was thinking or nervous. "That's not entirely true. There was only one room available, and she knew we'd divide the beds by gender. She also told me once that it's a good thing we have Frankie around so that we don't turn into a bunch of ex-military assholes who have no clue how to treat a woman."

That gave me pause. Frankie was the first woman—the only woman until Brea had come along—that I'd let into my heart after my mother had died. Really she was the only woman I'd known in strictly a friendship sense. Sure, I'd served alongside women, but I hadn't thought much about them as people. They'd been Marines, same as me. Once I'd joined the Marine Corps Forces Special Operations, women had ceased being part of my world—until Frankie had come along. Equal parts sass and kickass, she'd quickly earned my respect. Over time and through shared experiences, she'd become my friend.

I can't pinpoint an exact moment when it happened, just that it had. Much of the way I viewed women had to do with what Frankie had taught me about the fairer sex. Until her, I'd sought women who were

Michele Zurlo

submissive and feminine, the kind who wanted a strong, guiding hand and who were kind of helpless—women who were exactly like my mother. Through her example, Frankie had taught me that a good woman could be emotionally strong, smart, and opinionated. In a lot of ways, she'd prepared me to open myself to Brea, who was all of those things and more.

I cleared my throat. "She's right. Frankie, you keep us real. Without you, we wouldn't be half the men we are today. We'd be dicks."

"You still kind of are." Frankie delivered that with a smile.

"You're right, we are." Jesse got up and stretched, and he directed his next comment to me. "We've been treating her differently, in little ways, because she's a woman. It's time we made her one of the guys 100% of the time." He pulled a quarter from his pocket. "Best two out of three. Call it."

I jumped in the moment he flipped the coin into the air. "Heads."

Jesse caught the coin and slapped it onto the coverlet. "Tails. I win. Frankie, you're next." He tossed it again.

"Heads." She knew exactly what was on the line. Both Jesse and Dean had complained about me flopping my arms or legs over them in my sleep before.

The coin fell onto the coverlet. Frankie and Jesse watched it land, and Jesse grinned. "I like this new egalitarian side of you, Frankie." To me, he said, "Remember, she's no more open to snuggling with you than I am."

I lifted a brow at Frankie. "So, when are we meeting this new guy you're dating?"

She rolled her eyes. "I swear to God, if any of you chase this one off, I'll cut off your balls and ram them down your throats."

I went to her and rested my hands on her shoulders. Looking deep into her dark eyes, I said, "Frankie, I'll always be your friend. Rest assured that if he hurts you, nobody will ever find a body." Yeah, she might be a woman, but she was my friend, and nothing would deter me from looking out for her.

An hour later, our search for lunch led us to a local café that served kickass empanadas and a locally made microbrew. We chatted as we ate, keeping our voices low because we were actually checking out the patrons.

With his finger, Jesse scooped up some mashed potatoes and chilies that had spilled out. He licked his finger clean. "I saw more flyers with Rocha's face on them in the hall. He's sponsoring some kind of auto show."

Their server, a fifty-ish woman who strolled through the café no faster than a summer breeze, stopped at their table. Like most people in town, she was not in a hurry to go anywhere or do anything. She smiled and set down another plate of empanadas in front of me. "A *gran hombre* like you needs much food. For energy? Yes?"

The food was good, but I was almost full. Flashing my most devastating smile, I thanked her. "Whose picture is on the posters for the auto show?"

Her grin grew. "Carvalho Rocha. He is also handsome devil, like you. Senor Rocha is our patron. He pays for medicines in our clinic, and he buys books and uniforms for the school children in the village. Cadez is blessed to have him. He brought the auto show and all these tourists here."

"How wonderful!" Frankie's smile lit her face. "Has he always been such a generous patron?"

"Always." The server's smile softened. "Before he came here, our village was very poor. Our clinic did not have much medicine, and many children could not attend school. He came too late for me and my *ninos*, but my *nietos* are able to learn much."

"When was that? How many years ago?" Frankie tried to match the server's softer, reverent tone. She came close enough so that the server didn't notice.

The woman looked skyward, her lips moving as she counted. "Fifteen? This is *quince*?"

"Yes." I answered because, of the trio, I knew the most Spanish words. "That's wonderful. Maybe we'll have to come back next year for the auto show."

She went on to extol the virtues of the auto show, as well as several adventure packages aimed at tourists. After we finished eating, a tour of the town revealed an almost reverent attitude toward Rocha. The downtown area consisted of wide cobblestone streets, though motor vehicles were absent. I found this odd, considering flyers for the auto exhibition plastered every available surface. The stucco buildings surrounded a town square where enterprising local merchants displayed their wares.

Normally in an operation like this, we'd lay low. However this whole thing was already different, and doubt nagged at me. Cuyler expected us to get in and out quickly, leaving no trace. That's part of the reason we'd rejected Brea's plan—the one where Frankie sweet-talked her way into Rocha's place. Cuyler had all but suggested it first.

So we broke with protocol and wandered the town square. I'm glad we did. Everywhere we went, we caught snippets of conversation that confirmed our server's assertion. Carvalho Rocha was a very important and beloved figure in this town.

The next morning, we checked out of the hotel, making sure to mention the next destination on our list—one on the other side of San Tesoro. Frankie gushed about finally getting to see the ocean, and Jesse said he was looking forward to catching some waves.

"This takes me back." Jesse shifted his pack as he hacked branches and vines with a machete we'd picked up along the way. The rainforest wasn't as thick here as in some places, but we avoided the open areas because we knew they likely contained the odd farm or home. It was best to remain undetected.

"To what?" Unlike Frankie and Jesse, my service years hadn't taken me to the jungle. While theirs had, I didn't think it would elicit the nostalgia I heard in Jesse's voice.

Given the dense foliage and the thick, humid air, I wasn't sure this was much better than the desert. I slapped a mosquito trying to snack on my neck.

"My dad used to take us on long hikes, usually only a couple days, and once he took my brother and me to Brazil. We had a guide, and he got his jollies by taking us through the thickest parts of the underbrush." Jesse slashed at a vine. It fell into a big-leaf bush, and part of it slithered away.

Frankie snorted. "I thought you were going to bring up that time we chased Ahmed Abdullah from Libya to Colombia and got pinned down in the forest for almost six days."

Though Frankie and I also helped clear the path, we mostly kept watch for people, animals, reptiles, or bugs that could make our lives difficult. This jungle was probably not significantly different from the one in Colombia, yet Jesse chose to remember positive experiences. It was one way to keep the specter of our worst memories at bay.

"My dad once yelled at me for sending money to an organization wanting to save the rainforest." That's all I had to contribute.

Jesse groaned. "Way to ruin the mood." The foliage became suddenly sparse, and Jesse stopped short of exiting thick cover.

Frankie checked the GPS on a handheld device. "We're close to the location Cuyler gave us."

Using my high-powered, pocket-sized binoculars, I checked out the area. Still very forested, the topography rose sharply. We were at the base of the mountain. Rocha's place, according to the GPS, should be a half mile to the east. I panned in that direction, my eyes peeled for any sign of civilization. A house or a compound using as much power as Rocha would need to run his equipment was going to give off some kind of exhaust. A scan of the treeline showed nothing. I dropped my pack and motioned to the west.

Skirting the edge of the tiny clearing, careful to keep to the shadows, I sought a better vantage point. I found it on the other side of the clearing. There, the view to the south opened up. Tucked inside the recesses of a wrinkle in the mountain, I spotted a small, wispy cloud hovering just above the treetops. I couldn't see the house, but I knew it was there.

After creeping back to Jesse and Frankie, I pointed out my hunch on Frankie's GPS map.

"You're sure?" Jesse's eyebrows lifted.

"No, but I think it's our best bet."

Frankie pursed her lips. "It's not quite where Cuyler said it would be."

"True." I picked up my pack. "But his intel is incomplete. Whether on purpose or accident, I have no idea."

We didn't have a tight plan. We'd found that the tighter the plan, the more it was likely we'd encounter problems. Plans always went awry. It was best to be prepared for any likely—or unlikely—contingency. We spent the night discussing possible scenarios.

Early the next morning, we crept closer to Rocha's compound, familiarizing ourselves with the lay of the land and mapping escape routes. Mid-day found us with our eyes on a fantastically large, modern home set into the side of the mountain. Walls of glass overlooked what I guessed was a spectacular view.

Jesse pointed a thermal imaging device at the house. "I count four inside and another six guarding the perimeter."

"I like those odds," Frankie said. "But I don't trust them. He's a tech genius. There's no way he doesn't have a crap ton of digital security." She took my high-powered binoculars and climbed a tree for a better look.

I peered over Jesse's shoulder, and together we recounted the heat signatures indicating people. I pointed to a low-profile blob. "Looks like a medium-sized dog or a really big cat."

Without looking up, Jesse said, "Did you and Brea hatch a contingency plan in case something goes wrong?"

Today was Wednesday. We had one chance to get this right. "Yeah. I gave her a sack of cash and told her to disappear. I told her to take Jessica with her. Those two are experts at surviving together."

He exhaled. "Good. I'd hate to fail them, but that's a distinct possibility. I think the server room is set behind the house, in the mountain itself. Fuck if I see a good route inside. I wish Rocha was an imbecile, but he used the mountain to his advantage."

I also wished Rocha lacked intelligence. "No such luck."

The thump of boots, muffled by detritus material, landed beside me. Frankie handed back my binoculars. "No such luck what?"

"Rocha being an imbecile. If we can't carry out our mission, I've given Brea instructions to take Jessica and disappear." I tried to sound unconcerned, but Frankie saw through me.

She squeezed my arm. "We'll get it."

A high-pitched buzzing whizzed past my ear. If I hadn't seen combat, I would have assumed it was a tropical insect. But I couldn't forget my training. I grabbed Frankie and Jesse. "Down."

Another shot fired, and that's when I realized these were warning shots. Shit. We'd been spotted.

Brea: Seems Like Old Times

We landed in Abundante, San Tesoro's capital city and home of its international airport, early Tuesday morning. Using some of the cash David had left for me to flee, we rented a sand-colored, dinged-up secondhand car identical to the ones clogging the streets. Once we cleared the city, cars like ours, trucks, and busses were the only vehicles around. I gave us five stars for blending in. The last thing we wanted to do was look like tourists. Calling attention to ourselves would look suspicious to Charlie. He knew what we were, and I hope he wasn't still nursing a grudge for the way I'd left him fifteen years ago. Time healed most wounds, and the rest could be laid at the feet of BS.

"I'm not going to like the part where we pretend that BS is our father again." My lower lip trembled. I hadn't yet worked past the intense fury that gripped my gut when I thought of Brian Sullivan/Eugene Bowen.

Jessica, who had spent less time in denial than I had, glanced at me. "We left him because we wanted a different life. Charlie would buy that we've broken away from BS and want nothing to do with him. It makes the treasure hunting sound more plausible. I mean, what else are two reformed grifters going to do?"

She was correct. The twisting in my stomach eased. "He'll be more forgiving if he sees us as victims." We were victims of a con artist, grifter, and madman, but I didn't like to think of myself as a victim. I preferred David's term—survivor. As much as my shrink Nikki had helped me, David had helped me even more. His love and support gave me strength, courage, and protection. I loved David, and I was not going to allow Grayson Cuyler to tear us apart.

We made it to Cadez late Tuesday afternoon. Time was running short. We needed to find Charlie—I couldn't think of him as Carvalho unless he asked me to call him by that name—and convince him that treasure hunting was worth his while.

The auto expo was set up inside a huge warehouse on the outskirts of town. The outside had been transformed with paint, and a colorful marquee announced the show. Even though it wasn't open, I expected Charlie to be here. As the main sponsor, he would have wrangled special access to the venue. He'd want to be the first to see the cars, trucks, and motorcycles that would be featured. He'd want to schmooze with the engineers and models.

A good number of people thronged the street, mostly locals swarming out of the building after a day's work. I parked the car across the way a little past the warehouse entrance. Jessica opened the hood and poked around in the engine. Since she had no idea what she was looking at, I joined her to prevent her from doing irreparable damage.

"There's nothing wrong with the car."

She blinked at me. "But if there is, won't he stop to help us? I mean, two hot American women stranded in the street—he won't be able to resist."

"Not likely." I motioned for her to move her hands out of the way, and I closed the hood. "We need him to recognize us, and the hood being up will block his view." I spread a map over the hood. "Let's plot the best path to the treasure."

She retrieved the authentic-ish map from the journal she'd forged and opened it. "There." She pointed to a mountain, Mont Fresca. "It's the most likely spot."

We plotted for almost an hour as workers straggled out of the warehouse, but Charlie was nowhere to be found.

"It's not working." I folded the map which now bore circles and lines marking routes and destinations. "I want a closer look at those posters plastering the wall. If I'm not mistaken, the face on them looks familiar."

We crossed the street and stared at the posters featuring a color washed image of Charlie's face. This was the kind of picture where you had to know the featured celebrity or else the image was merely a human-shaped blob. I recognized the prominent cheekbones, full lips, and those warm brown eyes. Charlie and I had both been fairly innocent when I'd broken his heart. For the first time in my life, I hoped that he'd been conning me too.

A car pulled up. The sleek black SUV was new, expensive, and shiny, the opposite of the average vehicle in this area.

Jessica tugged at my arm as the door opened, already beginning the act. "This isn't what we're here for. We don't have time for an auto expo. We have real work to do."

Though we were improvising, I played along. "But there will be lots of locals there. We need to find a guide, or we're not going anywhere." I shook off her hold and stepped to my left, which meant I bumped into a big man on the outside of Charlie's entourage.

I teetered, and he steadied me. The hard expression on his face betrayed a lack of interest in me or Jessica. I put my hand on his biceps. *"Lo siento. Disculpame, por favor."*

He waved, dismissing both my thick Spanish accent and me.

Before his group could advance much farther, I gasped. "Charlie? Is that you?"

He paused, and in that half second of hesitation, I seized my chance.

"It's me—Ara. Arabella Bonano."

Surrounded by four bodyguards, he turned slowly.

The closest bodyguard, the one who'd been in the back, eyeballed me dispassionately. The one between Charlie and Jessica kept watch on her. The others scanned the area, no doubt looking for threats.

I swallowed, wetting my throat that had gone dry. "It is you, isn't it? Or have I totally stuck my foot in my mouth?" Despite spending most of the night and day traveling, Jessica and I appeared rested and fresh. A weary appearance would rob me of power, and I needed power in order to do this right.

He tapped his bodyguard—all of them were much larger than he was—and the man shuffled to the side. Charlie looked at me closely, studying me with the barest trace of a scowl. His gaze swept over my body, but he mostly looked at my face. "Arabella Bonano. I remember you being a few inches shorter. And your face was rounder."

When I'd known Charlie, I'd been shorter than him. Now, wearing simple tennis shoes, I could look him straight in the eye. I smiled shyly and thought of something embarrassing to force a blush. "I'm older now, no longer a fifteen-year-old girl. I've grown up. You've matured as well." His shoulders had broadened, and his features and body had filled out.

That caught him off-guard. His mouth fell open, but he got control before the reaction went too far. "You were nineteen when we met. I was twenty."

Inclining my head toward Jessica, I said, "Isa was eighteen at the time."

He looked at her, studying her with the same intense scrutiny. Then he grabbed my arm—firmly, but not roughly—and hauled me away from his entourage. "What game is this, Ara? I have no patience for false accusations. You were not a virgin when we were together. As I recall, you taught me a few things."

I sought to soothe his passionate nature. "I make no accusations, Charlie. I was fifteen. My father forced me to lie so he could get closer to your father. It wasn't the first time, and it wasn't the last." Here I looked away. The shame was real. "I've cut him out of my life. Isa and I both have. We're treasure hunters now. We're in Cadez because we're looking to hire a guide to take us into the Mont Fresca forest."

Shades of understanding through his eyes as he connected the dots. A shred of uncertainty remained. "But you are here, now, with me. Why didn't leave when you saw me? If what you're implying is true, those can't be pleasant memories for you."

I shrugged. "I have far worse. Nothing that happened was your fault, and I have good memories of you."

He pressed his lips together. "Your father ruined mine, and you used me. You pumped me for information that your father used to take everything from my family."

"I had no choice." In order for this to work, I needed his sympathy.

With a shrewd eye, he studied me. I let my vulnerabilities show.

I lowered my volume to a whisper. "It took us a few years, but we escaped from him."

"Did you?" His brows lifted.

"Six years ago." I looked to Jessica who stood a few feet away to give us privacy. "We keep moving, just to be safe."

Understanding and the beginnings of acceptance softened his eyes. "Still, seeing me can't be easy."

Easy—no. Necessary—yes. I sighed. "Charlie, you were the first man who treated me with respect. I—That's what I kept from my time with you. My fiancé respects and cherishes me. I held out for that because you showed me it was possible."

Yeah, I was laying it on thick, but not all of it was a lie. David had come a long way since we first met. And the rest...Charlie had been my sub. I'd demanded from him the things I had wanted most from a man—reverence.

Speaking of Charlie, he looked like he'd swallowed a walnut, shell and all. While I'd been lost in thoughts of David, he'd been processing what I was telling him. I touched his chest. "Charlie? Are you all right?"

"I'm sorry." He shook his head. "I am so sorry. Ara—I regret everything. When you left, I hated you. I cursed your name. I never again let a woman Top me. Even today, I knew it was you the moment I heard your voice. I thought about ordering my guards to seize you so that I could get revenge." He swallowed and looked up over the rooftops. "But it seems that you were the real victim. I am so sorry. Had I known...I wouldn't have...I wouldn't have blamed you. Please let me make it up to you."

I'd been afraid there would be residual effects of his broken heart. Jessica hadn't been exaggerating when she'd told David and the crew that I'd left Charlie in a pool of tears and snot. I shook my head. "You owe me nothing. I've waited years to explain and apologize to you. I never thought I would see you again. I went back to your father's home a few years ago, but everything was gone." Because my vindictive kidnapper had burned it to the ground.

"He passed away ten years ago, and I live here now." Charlie took my hands in his. "Let me help you find a guide. You and Isa will be my guests. Perhaps you will allow me to provide security on this treasure hunt? There are unscrupulous elements in these parts." He glanced toward Jessica, and then he peered up and down the street. "Where is this fiancé of yours?"

"He had to work, but he gave his blessing for Isa and me to come down here. He said that if nothing else, we'd get a tan and a nice vacation out of it." I smiled, thinking of David and how he'd shake his head if he knew that I was knee-deep in grifter's paradise. Okay, he'd do more than shake his head, but at the end of the day, he'd know there was nothing he could do to stop me.

Charlie mistook my smile, as I'd hoped he would. He shook his head. "You will accompany me to a private preview of the expo, and we will catch up. I'll treat you to dinner, and then you will stay in one of my luxurious rooms."

Throwing back my head, I let loose with a loud bout of laughter. When it died away, I swatted his arm. "You don't sound at all submissive. I think you've changed."

"Such things were necessary." He offered his arm, and I took it. He motioned to Jessica, and she joined us. "Now I have two *bonita* women to show off. This is a good day."

Inside the warehouse, the bodyguards gave us a little more room. The huge space was divided into smaller ones, an area cordoned off for each vehicle. The locals would never be able to afford those cars, and I wondered if there was another reason for the show.

"Call me Carvalho," Charlie said as he ran a reverent hand over a shiny red fender. "That's who I am now—Carvalho Ferreira Rocha, entrepreneur."

Jessica opened a car door and slid into the driver's seat. "Is there anything we should know? Topics to avoid?" It appeared we were still on the same page.

He chuckled. "No, but if I ask for privacy, do not be offended."

We spent a few hours checking out the cars. Jessica and I admired the interiors while Carvalho—formerly Charlie—raved about fenders and chassis. Dinner was a quiet affair at a local diner where everyone greeted Carvalho as if he was a celebrity. When our meal was served, they left us alone. Nobody asked him about us, though he did introduce us as friends from long ago. The drive back to his place—one of his guards drove our car because Carvalho insisted we accompany him—took a little over an hour.

As the SUV wound through a rough, tree-lined path carved from the forest, a rut jostled me into the guard sharing my bench seat. I'd given the one next to Carvalho to Jessica because I could tell her hip was hurting, and I didn't want her to go through the discomfort of having to climb into the rear seat.

I peered up at the man built like a serious wrestler and a bodybuilder had a baby. "Sorry."

He glanced at me and nodded, but he said nothing.

"I'm Ara."

Again, he nodded without speaking.

"Are you not allowed to talk? Carvalho, do you have your bodyguards under a gag order?"

Carvalho turned, peering back at us. "Though Diego is a man of few words, his wife does not like for him to befriend beautiful women."

I regarded Diego sympathetically. "My fiancé has my heart, so your wife has nothing to worry about. Don't worry. I won't force the issue. I wouldn't want to get you in trouble."

Diego did that brief nod again, but this time the corner of his mouth turned upward. This lack of communication did nothing to shorten the drive, and it was difficult to follow and participate in a conversation happening in a seat in front of me. Judging from the amount of chatter and laughter coming from that seat, I knew Jessica was working her charm on Carvalho.

Mostly, that was a good thing. She was giving Carvalho a chance to feel us out. The danger in that lay in playing the game too perfectly. They say you can't con a con, but that's not exactly true. It was possible, but it was exponentially more difficult. Jessica and I had worked on our cover for hours, going over details large and small. Our stories were not perfectly coordinated because no two people interpret a situation the same way. Though we didn't do it in real situations because that's not how our relationship worked, we knew how to bicker convincingly.

We arrived at Carvalho's house in the pre-dawn hours. It was far too dark to see much, but I had the sense of a grand and imposing structure.

Carvalho helped me from the car. "Welcome to my home. Raoul will show you to your chamber. When you arise, we will plan this treasure hunt. I will introduce you to a friend who knows these mountains well."

Jessica leaned against the side of the SUV. I looked her up and down. "Where is your cane?"

She motioned to our rental car, which had just pulled into the large, curving driveway. No words, but she winced.

Carvalho frowned. "Exploring caves and spelunking is serious business, Isa. Are you sure you should be doing this?"

She grinned through the discomfort. "Sitting for long periods is more painful, and nothing is going to keep me from finding this treasure."

"I'll get our things and your cane."

Carvalho stayed me with a hand on my wrist. He motioned to Diego. "The cane first, and then deliver their luggage to the west guest suite." Once Jessica had her cane, he parked a respectful hand on both of our lower backs. "I will show you the dining room and how to get to your suite."

He led us through a magnificent hall that opened into a stunning living room. One side was made entirely of glass, and it rose three stories. I stopped, openly gawking. "Carvalho, this is incredible."

"In a few hours, the sun will rise, and you will discover true magnificence." A pleased smile curved his lips.

Jessica pointed up to a series of balconies I hadn't noticed. "Those carvings are amazing. Is that all done by hand?"

"Yes. A couple in town made them. I prefer to hire local talent as much as possible." Flattery definitely made him preen. He went on to describe how he had collaborated in the creative process. He'd wanted one to feature birds and another that paid homage to the indigenous cultures of San Tesoro.

From where I stood, the carvings were impressive, but I couldn't see much detail. At last Carvalho led us to the back of the house, which was darker because the bottom two floors were set into the mountain. As we neared the stairs, a man dressed in green camouflage ran up to Carvalho. He spoke in rapid Spanish, but I deciphered enough to know that they'd caught intruders.

I fervently hoped someone else had the bright idea to break into Carvalho's house. If he'd caught David, Jesse, or Frankie, then he wasn't going to let them walk out the front door.

Carvalho's eyebrows drew sharply together, dark slashes that lent him an air of foreboding. He faced me. "Is there anything you wish to tell me, Ara?"

I glanced at Jessica. We hadn't prepared for this, but we were used to the unexpected. A thrill ran through me, and exhilaration chased away my fatigue. I covered it up with a scowl. "Those motherfuckers better not have followed us."

Carvalho crossed his arms and looked between Jessica and me.

Jessica's scowl matched my own. "Bounty hunters. We're, um, we maybe are suspected of...something." She wasn't being a flake. It was never good to come out and admit to committing a crime.

Silence stretched, and we let it continue. Finally Carvalho sighed. "I know what you have been, ladies. You will tell the truth now, or I will assume the worst."

My shoulders slumped, as did my buoyant mood. Jessica put a comforting hand on my arm. "It'll be okay, Ara." She turned the full force of her liquid green eyes on Carvalho. "We took a politician for eighty grand. He put a price on our heads. These bounty hunters have been after us for about six months."

Jessica's story, when combined with the things I'd shared so far, didn't quite mesh. Carvalho caught the mistake. He turned that scowl on me. "And this fiancé of yours, he is at home, working a normal job, and he has no idea who you really are?"

I glanced away guiltily. "He knows some things. There's no reason to tell him everything. He wouldn't understand."

Carvalho wrapped his iron grip around my arms and shook me. One of his bodyguards restrained Jessica. I felt Carvalho's hot breath on my cheek. "You are lying to me, Arabella. I could kill you for this."

"I swear I'm not lying to you, Charlie." I met his gaze. "I'm not telling the whole truth because I'm entitled to my secrets."

"Why are you here?" His question roared through the space, echoing from the tall ceiling, and his fingers dug into my flesh.

"Treasure." Jessica struggled against the bodyguard. "If we can find this treasure, we'll have enough money to disappear. We can pay off the bounty hunters, buy new aliases, and disappear. The bounty hunters know all our current aliases. These were our last. We haven't used these names in years, and we weren't sure if they were safe. It was a gamble." Her frantic gaze met mine. "We shouldn't have been seen in public like that. We should have been discreet. We shouldn't have come to his home."

I conjured a tear and let it leak from my eye. "Charlie, please—we have to see if it's them. I have to know if we can stop running." Carvalho, I knew, had been on the run for years. It's why he was stuck in Central America instead of moving freely through the US.

My pleas broke through. He released me slowly. "Wouldn't you prefer to identify the bodies?"

The thought of David dying made me ill. I might have gone a little gray—I certainly felt ashen—and Carvalho slipped an arm around my shoulders. "You've never been the bloodthirsty type."

We followed Carvalho and his phalanx of bodyguards down two flights of stairs and into a damp sublevel lit by several bare bulbs dangling from the ceiling. This was the underbelly of the beast, not a place one showed off to guests.

Surrounded by four more burly guards armed with sleek assault rifles, David, Jesse, and Frankie knelt on the floor with their hands bound behind them. They looked at us the moment we entered the room. Frankie was closest to the door. The only indication she knew us was the slight narrowing of her eyes. David's jaw tightened, and a vein in his neck ticked. Jesse's face betrayed nothing. Without trying to look obvious, I searched for signs of injury.

Frankie's shirt was torn, and dark stains on her side and shoulder showed where she'd bled. Additionally, her eye looked like it had taken quite a hit. Jesse's thigh bore the mark of a knife wound, and he was bleeding from cuts on his lip and near his hairline. David's jaw was mottled and swollen, and blood dripped from a wound above his left eye.

I stopped in front of David and fought the urge to free his arms and tend to his wounds. He looked up at me, a dangerous warning in those dark brown eyes.

Before I thought too hard about it, my hand flew out, and I slapped David's cheek. Hard. My handprint bloomed in white before blood rushed to fill it with vivid pink.

The foreboding expression on his face did not change. He spit blood at my feet. It splattered onto my shoes.

"You ruined my life and my favorite shoes," I hissed. I slapped him again and again until a hand stayed my aim.

"I will deal with this mess." Carvalho's soothing tones penetrated my pretend fog of rage. "You are free now."

I sniffed and wiped away the wetness from my cheeks. Jessica hugged me to her, and together, they led me from the room. "We need to question them," Jessica said once we were out of earshot. "We need to know if this was a contract deal or if there are more."

Carvalho nodded to a guard. "Secure them in separate cells." To us, he smiled gently. "Sleep tonight. They are going nowhere. There is time, ladies. You will have your chance at finding answers."

In the privacy of our suite, I sank down onto the soft, butter-hued leather sofa, and I put my head in my hands. "Isa, what are we going to do?"

She sat next to me and hugged me close. "We're going to get some sleep because we're running on fumes. In the morning, we'll interrogate those relentless bounty hunters. Once we know the full story, we'll be able to plan our next move. Honey, there's a real chance that we won't ever be able to go home."

I let loose a stifled sob, careful to keep my face covered in case there were cameras in the room. Though I was genuinely upset, I was hopeful, and I couldn't quite hide that emotion. We knew there were listening devices, and we made no move to mind or disable them. This was a test that we had to pass.

Rubbing my eyes reddened them, and I faced Jessica. "Jason will never understand. He won't give up his career to go on the run with me." I named my fictitious fiancé after a very attractive actor. David had come upon Jessica and me looking at a video of Jason working out. He'd teased me, and I'd teased him back by assuring him that it wasn't a real competition unless David grew dreadlocks.

Jessica's short burst of laughter could be taken as empathy. "Ara, then maybe he's not The One. If someone loves you, then things like that don't matter. I think that even if there are no other bounty hunters after us, once these guys are gone, Senator Mettings will simply hire someone else to neutralize us. We humiliated him."

I sighed. "But no one knows, not unless he's running around and shooting off his mouth."

She tugged at my arm. "There's no sense in worrying now. Let's see what tomorrow brings."

I followed her to where Raoul had set our suitcases out on a divan. As I selected a comfortable shirt for sleep, I grumbled. "I wanted to start looking for that treasure later today."

David: My Favorite Dark, Dank Cell

As far as dank and dark stone prisons went, this one was relatively clean. The lone, naked light hanging from the center of the ceiling left shadows in the corners, but I saw no sign of rodent droppings. Spiders and other creepy crawlies, however, had their run of the joint. Something with too many legs to count made its way over my right hand, which was bound over my left one behind my back. Nope, this was not even close to being the worst prison.

I learned forward so that I could shake the critter off before it left behind an itchy, infected bite. Once the thing was gone, I flexed my jaw. It had been a few hours since Brea had slapped me like a crazy woman. She hadn't left a lasting impression, but the guy who'd flattened me with a lucky left hook sure had.

A noise in the hall put me on high alert. I'd already tried to come up with a plan to break out of the room. Each of the scenarios I imagined required knowing what the hell Brea and Jessica were doing out there. I'd figured they were going by the aliases Jessica had mentioned—Isa and Ara, the Bella sisters, but that's all I could reliably infer. That, and the fact we'd done something to ruin their lives. Were they escaped fugitives, or were we a rival group of cons who wanted to settle a score?

I didn't know where Jesse or Frankie were being held, but I figured they'd ended up in similar circumstances. While Brea had been slapping me silly, Jessica had been whispering to Rocha.

Fixing a mutinous glare on my face, I readied myself for whatever Brea had planned. I had no doubt that she was responsible for whatever was going on right now. This reminded me a lot of when she'd Topped me, only I was under no illusion this would be enjoyable.

A man came in, a big dude wearing a tight shirt and loose pants. He pointed an M-16 semi-automatic assault rifle at me. "Get up."

I rose slowly, playing up all real and perceived injuries.

A second man brought in a chair, which he placed in the center of the room under the light. "Sit."

I sat, and I cooperated as they untied my hands only to handcuff my wrists to the slats in the chair and bind my ankles to the chair with leather cuffs. Though I looked for openings to escape, these guys were too good at what they did.

The second man tested my bonds, and then he called through the door. *"Senorita Bonano, entra."*

Brea came in. She sported a well-rested face and a bright smile that she aimed at the guards. *"Gracias, Diego y Fernando."* The smile vanished, and the brightness on her face turned to thinly veiled hostility as she cast her attention in my direction.

I let my gaze drop, and I openly admired the cleavage revealed by the vee of her teal tank top. The necklace she wore dangled there, and the charm disappeared into a place I wanted to bury my face.

She grasped my chin and forced my gaze to hers. "I will eat you for dinner, heartless bounty hunter. I'm your one chance of surviving this little vacation, and that will only happen if I like what I hear."

It took every ounce of self-preservation not to laugh. I toyed with the idea of suggesting that I might enjoy being eaten by her, and that I would enthusiastically reciprocate. My final decision was to say and do nothing.

Her eyes narrowed as she studied me. Finally she released my chin, and none too gently. "I see you understand the gravity of your situation." She turned to the guards. "You can wait outside. We're just going to sit in here and chat. Two old friends, shooting the breeze and catching up."

They exited, though before he closed the door, Diego or Fernando set a second chair inside the room.

Now that we were alone, she circled me. As far as intimidating moves went, hers was pretty darn good. If I didn't know her the way I did, her performance would have made me uncomfortable. Everything about her screamed "master interrogator." Even knowing her the way I did, I still half expected her to pull a knife out of her pocket and press the point against my carotid. She stopped behind me and leaned down. Her breath fanned my neck.

"This is so flipping hot. I'm thinking this could be a really cool scene: You, bound naked to a chair. Me, armed with a blindfold and anything else I want to torture you with." She inhaled and moaned, teasing me with her proximity and my inability to move.

I gritted my teeth to keep from responding. Her voice was low enough so that it wouldn't be picked up by the microphone in the camera, but my voice tended to carry, so I stifled my reply.

"God, this is heady stuff. Such a rush." She circled me again, and I noticed how nice her ass looked in her jeans. Leaning down in front of me, she purred into my other ear. "Do you think I could get Jesse, Dean, or Frankie to subdue and deliver you to me?"

"No fucking way in hell that's happening." My snarl came out loud and clear because my answer was versatile enough to work in many situations.

She chuckled. "Oh, my precious cupcake thief, you have really graduated from petty theft to the big leagues."

I growled and jerked, lunging for her as best I could, which didn't get me very far. "Stop playing games."

Backing off, she regarded me with her hands fisted on her hips. "They have images, but no sound. They can't hear us."

I glanced at the camera. "You can't be sure."

"I tried to fix it for them. It's not going to work for a long while." She dragged the other chair closer, turned it backward, and straddled it. "Still, we should be careful. I know you're not happy to see me here, but it's lucky for you that I came."

Lucky? She was lucky I was restrained. Otherwise I'd turn her over my knee and blister her ass.

"Carvalho thinks you're after Arabella and Isabella Bonano. He's agreed to hold you here until she and I escape."

"That doesn't help me achieve my goal." I was careful to maintain both my scowl and my alpha body language.

Brea watched me, her lips compressed into a thin line. "In a few hours, Carvalho, Isa, three guards, a local guide, and I are going to look for buried treasure. That leaves five guards in the house—one monitoring the cells, two in close proximity without a formal post, and two who monitor the perimeter of the house. The surrounding area is under digital surveillance, which is how they detected you in the first place. The housekeeper has the afternoon off. It's her granddaughter's birthday."

We'd swept for surveillance equipment, especially as we'd closed in on Rocha's compound. I shook my head. "There's something more."

"Probably. Carvalho is a tech genius. It's likely there's a lot more. Isa is discussing that with Jesse. We're going to do Frankie together."

That made sense, and we'd taken multiple steps to avoid any kind of detection equipment. I searched my memory, much as I'd been doing for the past several hours, on the hunt to identify every mistake.

"David, if you can neutralize the guards, you're home free. He relies heavily on technology, and law enforcement here is a joke. Just be gone before we return tonight."

She was so sure about her plan that I hated to point out the major flaw. "Sugar, what's your exit strategy?"

A little wrinkle appeared between her eyes. "Once we give up on the treasure, Isa and I will leave."

"But the bounty hunters, who are supposed to be after you, will have stolen a valuable hard drive and destroyed his servers." I let her draw the conclusion that suspicion would fall on her and Jessica, and that Carvalho wasn't likely to let her walk out of here alive.

She stood then, shoving the chair away. Then she slid onto my lap and cupped my face in her hands.

"What the fuck are you doing?" My heart beat so fast I thought it was going to explode. I'd been pinned down by terrorists and heavy fire, yet I'd never in my life been so freaked out. At the same time I wanted my hands free so that I could wrap her in my embrace.

"I think we were lovers before you decided I had other value. I think you're really after me because you've realized the error of your ways and you want me back. Perhaps your vandalism has to do with protecting me by seizing all evidence of my presence here." She shrugged. "And maybe Jesse has a thing for Isa. I'm not sure how to explain Frankie, but I'm willing to add her to us to create a threesome."

I sincerely had no response. Her plan was so far out there that I couldn't think of a single counterargument.

Her lips grazed mine, electric shocks set off in all direction. I couldn't move, and not because I was bound. "Have you completely lost your mind?"

"Yes," she purred. "Where you're concerned, I'm utterly crazy."

"Sugar—"

She cut me off by plunging her tongue in my mouth for a kiss that seared me despite the immediate and imminent danger. "Ara. Call me Ara. Or Autumn. That's a safe alias."

Despite her having been kidnapped and found, the alias was safe because the FBI had kept it quiet. They had no interest in investigating what Jessica and Brea had done when they'd been under the influence of their kidnapper. Their brother Leo had pulled strings to keep it out of the FBI press releases.

Though it was difficult to think with her kissing me, I recognized the fact that she was providing a distraction, and I forced my brain to take a fresh look at the situation.

I hadn't reacted with anger, hate, or malice when she'd slapped me.

None of us had appeared surprised to see Brea or Jessica here—because, in the backs of our minds, we'd expected them to make a move. We'd just hoped for one that led to self-preservation, not danger.

When they'd left a few hours ago, Rocha had lingered, studying me thoughtfully. He'd suspected that Brea and Jessica had been lying. It was imperative we feed him an alternative fact.

As I mulled, her lips returned to mine, and a piece of metal passed between us. A paper clip. Great. Hopefully my rudimentary lockpicking skills would hold up.

She pulled back and ran her hands over my chest and shoulders. "Leave me a love note. Tell me that I'm safe, that you've taken care of everything. That you'll leave clean passports in a locker at the airport, and you'll meet me in a non-extradition country. Maybe talk sweet or dirty in it."

"San Tesoro is a non-extradition country." Surely Rocha, a man stuck here because he was a fugitive from the law, would identify all the holes in this plan.

She did a combination snort and eye roll.

"You've ruined that for me, now, haven't you? Carvalho is an important man in these parts, and while he might not mind me sticking around, he's not going to look favorably on my former-bounty-hunter boyfriend hanging around town." She smacked a kiss on me one more time. "We could have had something great, David, had you not looked at me and seen dollar signs."

She knocked on the door, and it opened. Instead of Diego or Fernando, Carvalho Rocha stood on the other side, and he did not look happy. I wanted to be free so I could protect her from the strife coming her way. My muscles tensed, and I strained against my bonds.

She bounced from the room, a spring in her step, and I understood for the first time that she truly didn't need to be protected. This remarkable woman didn't need me to shield her from an international data thief with an eight-man guard detail—fourteen if the six guarding the perimeter got in on the action. She needed me to trust in her judgment and skill, and that's exactly what I would do.

Brea: The Hunt of a Lifetime

Riding a high I'd missed more than I'd thought possible, I faced Carvalho. With his arms crossed and that firm slant to his brow, he didn't appear nearly as thrilled.

Fernando and Diego went into the cell housing David, and I clapped my hands to my chest. "That was amazing, Carvalho. I got a little from him—we had a great first session—but I know there's more. Can we keep them for a couple more days? That'll give us a chance to go looking for the treasure, and I won't have to worry about anything."

His hard look turned dangerous. "That looked nothing like an interrogation."

I drew back and feigned shock. "Keeping a target off balance is always a good interrogation strategy."

"You were making out with him."

This time, I rolled my eyes. "Waterboarding doesn't work. My way is so much more pleasant."

"Ara, don't play games. Do you not have a fiancé? I demand to know the truth about your association with that man." He grasped my arm and led me upstairs. At least he hadn't thrown me in a cell. That was a good sign.

Taking this tactic had been a gamble, but I was an expert in making gambles pay off. "Is Isa still in with one of the others? I really wanted to debrief with her before we decide who is going to take on the last one."

Carvalho said nothing as he escorted me to a large room full of leather furniture and banks of dark computer screens. Smaller tech was scattered throughout. This room did not afford him much of a view, not like his living room did. It was where he probably did most of his hacking.

I scanned the setup before taking a seat. "I forgot you liked computers. I'm not much of a techie myself, but I learned how to use a spreadsheet a few years ago. I also find the internet useful in research, though nothing replaces a library and interviewing people who are descendants of natives."

He settled on a sofa across from mine, a deceptively pleasant smile on his lips. "The full story. Now."

"I've told you everything." If I gave it up too quickly, he'd never believe me.

"Ara, I know that when you pretended to have feelings for me, all those year ago, it was part of a con. I forgave you fairly quickly because I found out that you had no choice in the matter. I was, of course, completely unaware of your actual age." Thankfully he didn't sound as if he felt guilty. I did not want to take the chance that he might feel like prey. That could make him extremely dangerous.

However I understood the card he was playing. I lowered my gaze and looked away, rubbing my palms together nervously. "David and I were lovers." I swallowed. My voice had caught at the idea that David being my lover could be past tense. "A mutual acquaintance introduced us, and we hit it off. It was a whirlwind romance. Before I knew what had happened, I'd fallen for him."

Here I summoned a bittersweet sigh.

"You have a fiancé." He prompted me when I didn't go on.

"Jason. He's everything David is not. His idea of a good time is an evening at a sports bar watching a game and drinking light beer." Regret. That was the appropriate emotion to insert here. I regretted the way I'd betrayed Jason just now, and I regretted becoming engaged to someone wholly unsuited to be my husband. I met Carvalho's gaze. "He's a good man. He's never once looked at me and noticed the price on my head."

Silence rang out as Carvalho studied the conflicted emotions flickering across my face. Finally he shook a finger at me. "You still love the man downstairs."

There was no sense in denying it. "But I can't have him. He's like peanut butter, and I have a fatal allergy."

"What do you wish me to do with this lethal temptation?"

I knew exactly what he was asking. "Don't kill him. I'd rather spend the rest of my life outrunning him than to lose him completely. Just keep him here for a few days—long enough for Isa and me to get away, hopefully with some treasure."

He rose and went to a cupboard along the wall behind him. I recognized the bag he extracted.

"You went through my things." My outrage was unfeigned, even though I'd expected him to do exactly this.

Ripping open the zipper, he threw the bag at my feet. "Almost five thousand in cash."

"Eight thousand," I countered. "Unless you or one of your men got greedy. That's everything we have, which isn't enough to take us far."

"You stole half a million from a Miami drug dealer."

I had no idea how he knew about that, but there was no use in denying it. "That was years ago."

Carvalho shook his head. "Something is not right. I don't believe your story."

By way of response, I glared. The door opened, admitting Jessica and Diego. From her body language, I deduced that she'd been escorted here the same way I had been.

She crossed her arms and stuck out one hip. "What's going on here? I thought we were going to question the last man together?"

So she'd gone to Frankie instead of to Jesse as I'd assumed. Chicken.

Carvalho motioned to the sofa. "Please sit. We were just talking."

I patted the cushion. "Charlie doesn't care for my life's story."

She snorted and flopped down next to me. "Neither do you. Unfortunately we haven't come across a time travel device that would enable you to go back in time to have a serious discussion with your younger self."

Diego took up a post near the door. I couldn't help but notice the huge gun slung over his shoulder or the ones holstered at his side and on his thigh. He probably had one or two smaller ones hidden under his clothes.

Emboldened by the presence of his armed guard, Carvalho stood and clasped his hands behind his back. Perhaps he meant to seem intimidating, but the pose was subconsciously submissive. He faced us with a severe frown. "Your timing is too coincidental."

Jessica and I exchanged a questioning glance, and then she scowled at him. "Explain."

While I didn't scowl, I did frown. "I'd also like to know what that means."

"It means I have business tonight, and your arrival, as well as that of your friends downstairs, is not at all convenient. I am not a believer in coincidence."

Jessica shot to her feet and she faced Carvalho with her hands firmly on her hips. She leaned forward to intimidate him, but she didn't move closer. My sister knew exactly how far to push someone. "Look, I don't know what you've got going on, but we haven't asked to be part of it. I know Ara wants you to keep those three locked up while we go looking for treasure, but if it's easier to get rid of them right now—"

"No." I interrupted quietly, forcefully. "We've never killed anyone or been responsible for their deaths. That's not a line I'm willing to cross."

She stared at me, her lips pressed into a thin line. "We need that treasure. How else will we be able to afford to disappear? Starting over isn't cheap."

Cogs turned behind Carvalho's dark eyes as he processed our dispute and fit it into the story I'd spun. "Enough." He cut off our disagreement. "We will delay the search for a few days."

I shot to my feet. "Unacceptable."

"Once my business is concluded—"

I knew what his business entailed. And while I didn't care if he exposed scandals related to dozens of high-ranking politicians, I did care if Grayson Cuyler came after me. Before Carvalho could finish his thought, I cut him off. "Your business and our business are separate things. You can stay here and do your thing. Isa and I only asked for a guide. That's all we need from you. And if you don't want to recommend anyone, then we'll go back to town and hire our own."

He recognized our determination, and he would ascribe our desperation to our need for funds via the discovery of treasure. He nodded solemnly. "Diego, have Raoul ready my things. It appears I am going treasure hunting today."

My frown didn't fade. "What about your business? We can search without you just fine. We're not amateurs. This is what we do."

This time his smile was soft. "I cannot have you traipsing through my jungle unescorted. I will make time to do both. We will return at sunset."

Not if I had anything to do with it.

Three hours later found us deep in a Central American forest. My backpack contained trekking supplies and fresh water. In her backpack, Jessica carried the map and the forged journal, and she leaned on her trusty cane with the secret sword inside. Diego turned out to be our guide, which meant he was now speaking to me. Carvalho followed behind us, with two of his bodyguards rounding out the crew.

Diego pointed to a place where the underbrush thinned. "This trail leads to a waterfall sacred to our people."

Jessica pulled out her map where she'd circled locations that matched descriptions from the journal. "Which people are yours, Diego? Nothing specific was mentioned in the journal."

"The Pima. We are native to this region. Much of our culture has been lost, but we have retained some legends and customs. In town, we have a small museum dedicated to preserving what is left of the Pima." He set his pack down and studied the map. It didn't take him long to find our location. He stuck a finger at the map. "There. We are about five kilometers from your nearest location. The forest is thick there. What do you hope to find?"

Jessica shrugged. "Remnants of a Spanish gold mine could mean anything, up to and including gold. The journal mentions stealing and hidden caches, but what's in them isn't detailed."

"We're hoping for gold," I added.

Carvalho gestured to Jessica. "Isa, how can you be sure of these locations? Is the journal so very specific?"

"No. I guessed based on physical and geographical descriptors." She patted the pouch where she kept the journal safe from the elements. Plus I used the crude map Baeza drew."

"I'd like to see the original journal." He held his hand out.

Jessica shot me a sour look. "Not out here. I have it wrapped and sealed against the damp. Tonight, when we get back, I'll let you read it."

She turned away, and I took Carvalho's hand. "The journal is valuable as well. That's why we marked everything on the map."

He seemed to accept that, and we continued. Diego, for his part, became more talkative in his role as a guide. "The Pima have long been a peaceful people. We value a hard day's work, community involvement, and family. According to legend, when the Spanish came through, the Pima elders welcomed them at first. Before long, they had enslaved my ancestors, forcing them to work plantations. After a time, the Pima mostly escaped into a forest. They hid in caves and learned to live in trees."

My heart went out to his ancestors. I wanted to hug the entire town of Cadez, but I didn't think my empathy would go over very well. I glanced back at Carvalho who frowned thoughtfully as he looked up at the canopy.

I kept an eye on Carvalho, but I directed my question at Diego. "They learned to live in trees?"

"Yes. Some of the plants here form cups or bowl-like structures that collect water. It is possible to stay off the ground for long period of time." He continued talking, imparting stories passed down through the generations, and I kept one eye on Carvalho and the other on Jessica. This strenuous hike might prove to be too much for her.

Several hours later, we found the first spot on the map. It was overgrown with lush jungle vegetation, just as Diego had said.

"This isn't our best bet," Jessica said. "It's just the closest location mentioned in the journal. Baeza mentions that his partner was murdered here." She tugged at my backpack. "It looks like your clasp came loose."

Carvalho surveyed the immediate area. Through the trees, we heard the hiss of a waterfall. "They probably stopped for water and were ambushed by the Pima." He pointed in the direction of the sound. "No way you're finding a body after all this time, but I suggest searching closer to water."

He had a point. People were easier to ambush when they were squatting down to refill a canteen. Still, I didn't want to give in too easily to the man who held David's life in his hands. I was feeling a passive-aggressive urge that would not be denied. Plus Jessica's concern had actually been a message.

"Let's search this area first." I took out a sonic imager—the item Jessica had put in my bag when she'd noted that the clasp was loose—that I'd stolen from Jesse's office. I figured that since I was using it to save his life, this didn't violate my promise to stop breaking into people's offices and taking things without their permission.

"What's that?" Carvalho leaned closer to check out the screen.

"Sonic imaging device. It should tell us if anything is buried here." I had no idea how. Technology like this was not my strong suit, but I figured that Carvalho would buy our treasure hunter cover story better if we had serious stuff. Plus, it would be cool if we found something treasure-ish.

I flipped a switch, hoping that was how this thing turned on. Since Jesse had fabricated the scanner himself, he hadn't labeled anything. Nothing happened. Jessica pushed a button on the top. "Ara, I love when you try to look like you know what you're doing."

The device came to life. Colors flashed across the screen, and it made a static-y sound. "I know how to use it," I protested. "We just haven't had it in the field yet. It's a virgin."

Carvalho lifted two dark, skeptical eyebrows. "You stole it?"

I nailed him with my witheringest glare. "I liberated it from someone who won't miss it." He wouldn't know at all, not until I came clean, anyway, which I would do because Jesse deserved the truth.

The scanner part was easy to find. I pointed it at the ground.

"I still say closer to the waterfall is a better place to look." Carvalho's mouth turned down in a petulant pout.

"We will," Jessica assured him. "But this location was mentioned in the journal. Baeza had been stealing from the Spanish. He buried his earnings in several possible places. It's important to leave no stone unturned." She turned to him to find that he was still pouting. "Seriously? Do I need to turn you over my knee?"

I'd followed Carvalho's actions closely—as well as those of bodyguards/guides Diego, Juan, and Jose—and I couldn't help but crack a smile at the method Jessica had chosen to subdue Carvalho. I'd burned that bridge with him, but she hadn't.

"If that is what you wish." He flashed a wolfish grin, but the pout disappeared.

Since she was handling him, I scanned the ground. Though I fully expected to find nothing of value, I maintained a hopeful expression. I stepped around a rather large tree, and the pitch on the scanner increased. As I mapped the area, it screamed wildly to delineate the boundary of the find. Unfortunately it didn't also give us a 3D image of what was down there.

"You found something." Diego had stuck close to me, and now I heard his awe.

"It could be nothing." I didn't want to get his hopes up that we'd found treasure. "The accounts don't say Baeza buried the gold, only that he hid it somewhere." And I wasn't sure this thing picked up metal as much as it found anomalies in the density of the soil. "This could be a big rock."

He studied the scan. "After the insurrection, I spent years searching for missing people. Most of those we recovered were in shallow graves."

I wasn't well versed in the problems or history of this area, but I knew that parts of San Tesoro were still in conflict. However I did recognize the way his tone hardened. His search had likely been motivated by personal loss. I wanted to offer my sympathies, but I didn't think he'd take too kindly to me pointing out that I saw an emotion he was trying to hide.

I knelt down and began clearing away loose brush and detritus material. The humus layer, absent anything tamping it down, came away fairly easily. Once I hit harder packed dirt and a big-leafed bush got in my way, I looked up at Diego. "I didn't think to pack a shovel. I thought we'd be looking for cave entrances."

Juan and Jose, both cut from that strong, silent security specialist mold, each unfolded travel shovels like it was a competition, they accomplished it quickly, and two shovels plunged into the ground on either side of me. Their expressions dared me to ask them to do the heavy work.

Jessica, who had begun earnestly leaning on her cane about an hour into the hike, took up one shovel. I got to my feet and grabbed the other. "Thanks."

I wished digging in the forest was as easy as it was on TV, but there was no production crew to till the soil. After twenty minutes, Diego and Jose took a shift, and then Carvalho and Juan followed suit. We all worked together to uproot a huge bush. When Jessica and I took over for a second time, she struck something hard. I rooted around, looking for edges. If they were there, then we were most likely dealing with a buried rock.

"Please tell me they didn't bury a bunch of bombs around here." I muttered as I prodded.

"Not here, but they did on some of the plantations." Diego used his hands to scrape away the next layer of earth. "Don't buy a plantation that has been dormant for the past twenty years, no matter how beautiful the house."

I glanced at Carvalho as we abandoned the shovels and used our hands. "We hadn't planned to make this our home base."

Carvalho didn't react. He was probably glad we were here temporarily. I didn't know the full range of his business interests, but his father had been into smuggling arms and cocaine, all of it packaged in coffee to throw off search dogs.

"I found something." Carvalho lifted an object and brushed off the dirt. It looked like a small bone, though I wasn't sure which it was or what species could claim it.

We all checked it out. From the silence, I gathered that none of us knew what to make of it.

124

"It doesn't look human." Jessica spoke slowly, her statement almost a question. "What kind of animals do you have out here?"

"It's buried too deep." Jose lifted out another bone. This one was longer. "We'd need a forensic specialist to tell us if it's human or not, but this looks like a femur."

Jessica snorted. "I thought lemurs were only on Madagascar."

I sat back, laughing. "Isa, he said femur, as in leg bone." What she'd said wasn't that funny. The stress of the day was beginning to get to me. Pulling a con on Carvalho was not a big deal, but not knowing if Jesse, Frankie, and especially David were safe—that stretched my nerves the way little else had.

Jessica extracted something squarish. "You're getting goofy, Ara. I think you need to eat."

Carvalho exposed the top of a round, white thing that might be a bone. "I'm not heading home right now. Did we pack provisions?"

"*Si, Senor.*" Jose backed away from the deepening pit. "I'll get a fire started."

I felt a little like an archeologist, and I half wondered if we shouldn't be using brushes and dentist tools—things designed to uncover artifacts without damaging them. "Be careful. We don't want to damage anything."

"This could be the remains of a missing person," Diego added. "Thousands were never found."

Before long, the object was free, and I realized it wasn't a bone. The head-shaped item turned out to be a helmet with a crest running from front to back.

"It's a morion." Jessica took it from Carvalho to examine it closer. "Spanish conquistadors wore these beginning in the late 1500's."

"Actually," I added, "most soldiers wore them. That's why armies started wearing uniforms, because they couldn't tell friend from foe."

"It's iron. Did they have iron back then?" Carvalho knocked on the surface. "It's rusted through on some of the edges."

Jessica snorted. "Explorers found and exploited the Western hemisphere long after the Iron Age was but a distant genetic memory."

"So this is real?" Carvalho's eyes lit. "It's not very rusty for something that might be five hundred years old."

"They coated iron in tin to stop corrosion." Jessica supplied. "It could very well be from a Conquistador."

I shrugged. "Maybe. It'll need to be authenticated. Isa, the journal didn't mention a grave in this spot. Didn't it say a portion of the treasure was maybe buried here?"

"It indicated that this could be a spot." She frowned. "And the scanner indicated a larger area of disturbance."

"I say we keep digging." I looked at each member of our party, checking with Juan and Jose even though, technically, they were supposed to be there as bodyguards for Carvalho.

"Dinner is ready," Jose said. "Jerky and condensed soup. I suggest we take a break."

We separated temporarily to take care of private business. When we came back together, Jessica and I found ourselves alone with Jose. Next to the languid stream fed by the petite waterfall, Carvalho spoke with Diego and Juan. He gestured wildly, but since we were closer to the water than to them, his words were drowned out by the tinkle of the water falling over rocks. It wasn't a tall waterfall—maybe ten or twelve feet—but it made enough noise.

"How late did you want to stay out?" I directed this to Jessica. "I brought a tent on my frame pack."

"We have enough for breakfast, but not for lunch." She chewed as she thought. "We got a really late start today. How about we explore until nightfall, camp out, and see if we can catch some fish or a small creature in the morning? I saw some wild avocado, plantain, and breadfruit."

"We passed guava and cashew trees as well." Jose spoke slowly, his English heavily accented. "As long as we stay close to the stream, we can survive out here for weeks."

In one way, that sounded like paradise. On the other hand, it seemed like hell. I wanted to reunite with David sooner rather than later. "Isa and I only have a few days. This is kind of a last ditch effort to fund our disappearance. We have an unhappy Senator and at least one group of bounty hunters on our tail."

A hand clamped onto my shoulder. When I looked up, Carvalho flashed a sympathetic grimace. "Then we will look for a few days. Unfortunately we will need to return to my home tonight. I regret that it is necessary. Tomorrow we will set out again in search of buried treasure. You have lit a fire in me, Ara, with this exciting find."

Jessica started at this pronouncement. "We can't abandon this find. What if there's more than a Spanish helmet? The scanner indicated a larger area."

I could see where she was going with this. Staying here, even without Carvalho and his guards, would convince him once and for all that we were here for a treasure and nothing more. However if we parted ways now, we would have no control over how long it took for the return journey, and if things went sideways, I wouldn't be in a position to help David, Jesse, or Frankie.

"We can mark it." I glanced around at the darkening forest. "It'll be here tomorrow. Nobody knows where this is or that we found it."

Jose sat very still, and he spoke calmly. "Snakes in these parts hunt at night. Coral snake, pit viper, Yellowjaw—or Fer-de-Lance. That last one is grumpy and aggressive. By the time we get you to the hospital, you're likely to lose a limb. Then there's the spiders. We have an abundance of brown recluse and black widow spiders, poisonous centipedes, even scorpions in some parts." Though Carvalho didn't appear to be involved, I knew he was pulling the strings.

I didn't scare easily. While I didn't care to lose a limb to necrosis, my mind was made up. Jessica was the one who needed convincing.

She looked down, appearing to be thinking, but I knew she was looking at her hip and leg. In my single-minded pursuit of saving the others, I had forgotten how difficult this was on Jessica. She'd hiked a challenging, makeshift path today. Not only was she exhausted, but she had to be in pain. "You're right. I think I'd prefer a bed tonight."

Lumbering to her feet slowly, she picked up her cane and grimaced. I went to her and put my arm around her waist. "You pushed yourself too hard today, and I let you."

Michele Zurlo

She leaned against me. "I think maybe I mistook a lamp post along the way for the light at the end of a tunnel."

We made our way back to Carvalho's slowly, the journey back taking nearly twice as long. My heart welled with love for my sister, and I accepted that being a con was as much a part of me as she was.

David: Sometimes I Wish I Was MacGuyver

The paperclip didn't work the way I'd hoped. When the guards came in after Brea had left, they didn't untie me and remove the chair. Instead, they exchanged crude jokes about Brea, slapped my face a few times, and left. I guessed they thought with my hands and feet bound, I wasn't going anywhere.

I turns out they were correct. Although I gave it my best effort, the paperclip slipped noiselessly to the concrete floor. Picking locks was not my strong suit. Perhaps it was time I sucked it up and asked Brea to help me master these skills. If I could master the disarming of various types of bombs, then I could learn something this basic.

I scooted my chair to position my hand closer to where the paperclip had fallen, but the handcuffs prevented me from being able to reach the floor. If I broke my hand, I could free myself. It would need to be my left hand because I was right-handed. Taking a deep breath, I prepared to pitch the chair so that I fell on my hand.

A noise in the hall paused my plan. It wasn't loud—no shouts, thumps, or a stampede of running feet. That's what caught my attention. When things are copacetic, guards don't care about their volume. When things went awry, people got quiet. A second later, the door to my cell opened, and a head poked inside.

Frankie grinned, her dark eyes sparkling with excitement. She dangled a key ring. "Look what I found."

I nodded behind her. "The guards?"

"Two down. I locked them in my cell." She crouched behind me, trying different small keys. "If three are with Ara and Isa, that leaves three to go. David, if you don't marry that woman, I just might."

I thought about the way Brea gushed over Frankie's beauty, and I grew defensive. "Don't say that. I'm going to marry her as soon as we get back. Where's Jesse?" The handcuffs fell away, and I rotated my wrists. "Brea came to see you too?"

"No, Jessica—Isa—did. She had fun with it, and she's brilliant at asking the right questions." The right questions, meaning she communicated covert information effectively. Having freed my feet, she stood. "Let's find Jesse and get out of here."

Besides a few bruises on her face, Frankie didn't look the worse for wear, though I knew she was hurting. Based on the fight that had brought us here, I guessed at deep bruises and a possible concussion. The guard who'd taken her down had used a stun gun after she'd neutralized his friend.

We hurried down the hall. The cell next to me was empty, but the one after that contained Jesse. His eyes lit when he saw us. Unlike they'd done with me, the guards had chained Jesse to the floor. Thick manacles encircled his wrists and shackled his feet.

Frankie searched for a likely key while I examined Jesse's wounds. Of the three of us, he'd been injured the worst. In addition to numerous contusions, he had a gash along the hairline above his forehead and another on the back of his neck. The skin around his wrists was scraped raw, and I guessed that his ankles hadn't fared much better.

"Jessica, Brea—are they okay?" Jesse's voice scraped from his throat, a raspy whisper that indicated more damage to his neck than a deep cut.

"They're fine." I frowned. "Didn't one of them interrogate you?"

"No." He closed his eyes briefly. "Nobody's been in here except to bring me some water and a power bar, but that was hours ago."

"They're going by Isa and Ara Bonano." Frankie found the key that unlocked the shackles on Jesse's ankles. "We're bounty hunters who have tracked them here."

Jesse chuckled. "That's how she plans to get away with smacking the shit out of you. Ah, well. It's better than being treated like you don't exist."

I felt bad for Jesse. Not only had Jessica done nothing to acknowledge him—a safe move on her part—but she'd chosen to interrogate Frankie instead of putting Jesse's mind at ease. But like Frankie, I buried that emotion for a later time. We had a mission to carry out. "Ara and I are former lovers, and there's a good chance we reconnected during the time she questioned me."

Jesse's brain worked fast, but Frankie was even quicker. "We're going to erase evidence of them ever having been here, then the two of you are going to run off together."

"With new identities," Jesse added. "Since they're wanted. Are you running off with them both?"

I shrugged. "I can't very well leave the sister of my beloved behind." Anyone who knew Brea understood how much her sister meant to her. When I'd brought her to Kansas City to live with me, I'd brought Jessica as well.

Frankie freed Jesse's feet. "Feel sorry for yourself later. We have three guards out there to neutralize, a server to steal, and a fire to set."

That was Grayson Cuyler's plan, not ours. We helped Jesse to his feet. "No fire. Let Rocha keep his older information. We'll take his newest two servers, and I'll leave a note telling Ara to meet me near the airport so we can be together. Or some such romantic crap like that."

From the hard press of Jesse's lips, I figured that he was going to argue my changes. He was as invested in making sure Jessica was safe as I was in seeing to Brea's security.

I held up a hand. "I'm not burning this bridge. Rocha deals in information, and there might come a time when we need him for something. My gut tells me that Rocha has dirt on Cuyler, otherwise Cuyler wouldn't be so insistent on the place being destroyed."

"You trust Rocha?" Frankie's incredulity came through loud and clear.

"Not any more or less than I trust Cuyler." I pressed myself against the wall next to the door. "But there's no good reason to destroy this place."

Jesse halted our attempt to leave the room. "Where is Rocha right now?"

"Treasure hunting with Isa and Ara Bonano, three bodyguards, and a local guide." Frankie twisted the doorknob. "Let's get this done."

This was the kind of operation for which we'd been trained, and it brought with it a certain level of comfort with what had to be done. I cleared the corridor, and Jesse followed me out. We made our way upstairs, navigating by instinct. Careful to remain stealthy, we searched the main floor. Though we found two guards patrolling the perimeter, we did not take them down. The third must be watching the monitors, so we made our way to the rear of the mansion.

I felt it as we neared—the electromagnetic field created by massive amounts of power being channeled to one location. It tingled across my skin and left a metallic taste on my tongue. At least it wasn't like going past a high tension wire, where it felt like a vise was squeezing my chest and my nerves frayed to the breaking point.

I motioned to it, and Jesse nodded. Frankie took point, and I followed. The guard had been watching external security, so he hadn't noticed our movements through the house. Though we'd been careful, we weren't sure where every camera was located. If Rocha was a rogue tech genius, then he was probably a paranoid conspiracy nut to boot.

Wrapping one arm around the guard's neck, I took him down with a sleeper hold before he could figure out what was happening. Frankie held up a box of zip ties, mischief glowing in her eyes. I dragged him from the security room to a storage closet down the hall, and then I helped Frankie secure him to a rather large pipe that was probably the main sewage line. If he managed to free himself, raw sewage would spew all over, and we'd smell him before we saw or heard him.

Before heading outside to neutralize the remaining two guards, we checked in with Jesse. With a look and a gesture, he motioned for us to go. The security hub was connected to the server room, and he was going to stay behind to work his magic.

The guards patrolling the perimeter stood together on the massive deck overlooking the lush forest below. Armed to the hilt, they rested their hands on their weapons as they chatted. To the west, the sun was beginning to set. This presented a problem for Frankie and me because it was in our eyes.

Crouching low, we crept closer. It was a gamble because this was a fairly open spot. Though we didn't make a sound, one of the guards happened to turn his head.

"*Detener!*" The man pointed his M-16 at us as he turned.

Frankie and I had already committed to the takedown, and guns weren't the most effective weapon inside twenty-five feet. As one, we leaped. With practiced precision, she took the one on the right, while I targeted the one on the left.

My guy used his gun as a bat and took a swing at me. He expected me to block it, but I dove forward, threaded my arm between his arms and face, and wrapped his arms up in mine. While his arms were immobilized, his face was in perfect punching position. I delivered a few harsh blows. I didn't know if this was the fucker who'd messed me up and I didn't care. He was going to pay for roughing me up. He struggled against my hold, almost breaking it, so I switched tactics and kneed him in the gut until he vomited.

Now I had the gun, and I pointed it at his head. Breathing hard, I glanced at Frankie to find her standing over a prone body. "Is he dead?"

"No, but he's going to have one hell of a headache when he wakes up. Let's get these lovely gentlemen to a safe place."

I motioned to the guard who wasn't passed out. "Do you want to walk, or do you want to be carried?"

He lurched to his feet and lunged at me. I slammed the butt of the gun into the side of his head and he crumpled.

Frankie *tsked*. "He could have just asked to be carried. Such a baby."

We dragged them into the house and secured them in a back bedroom. All-in-all, they were each more comfortable than we'd been in captivity. That was part of the plan—not to make it too bad on them because my gut told me that being on speaking terms with Rocha could come in handy one day.

"I'll take first watch. You check in with Jesse." Without waiting for me to reply, Frankie headed to the balcony. Garbed in combat gear, from a distance nobody would figure her for a woman, which would be the first indication to Rocha that his security had been compromised.

I found Jesse tapping on a handheld device he'd connected to the private server. The stacks of hard drives reminded me of that old movie, Desk Set, where they installed a 60's-era computer into a huge room and it took up mountains of space.

"Wow—that's a lot of data." I walked the room, looking for anything that might be of concern.

When I returned to Jesse, he glanced at me. "It's not full. He has tons of space."

"That should make it easier to find the data we need."

From Jesse's frown, I gathered that I'd made a naïve statement.

"Do you need help with anything?"

"Check on the guard that used to be in here. I think he might be trying to break free."

I hustled down the hall to the small storage room to find our prisoner in a pile of paper goods. He'd knocked down a shelf containing napkins, toilet paper, and tissue. His wrists and ankles were still bound to the sewer main, but he was too mobile, and this room provided too little protection. Careful to keep my gun pointed at the man's head, I dug him out of the pile and cut his bonds. Then I tied his hands and ankles together, picked him up, and slung him over my shoulder. It had been a while since I'd done this, and I grunted under his weight. After all, the guy was nearly my height, and he had a powerhouse build.

"Fucking Americans. Coming into our country and taking things from us." He kicked and nearly slid from my shoulder.

I paused and repositioned him. "I'm going down the stairs. If I drop you, it's going to hurt you far more than it'll hurt me. In fact, it won't hurt me at all because I'll likely just shoot you to put you out of my misery."

He didn't stop fighting, and by the time I got to the bottom of the stairwell, I was barely holding onto him. I let him fall. He tucked and rolled, and then he fought back. Being tied up doesn't prevent someone from fighting back. I'd bound Brea's wrists and ankles before, and she liked to fight, so I had a few tricks up my sleeve. Of course I had no interest in sleeping with this guy, so I wasn't as nice.

I kicked him in the kidney. As he writhed in pain, I grasped him by the back of his jacket and dragged him into the cell once occupied by Jesse. "I tried to be nice, mister. We don't want to hurt anyone. We just want the fugitives we came for, and then we'll be gone." I double-checked the zip ties we'd used, and as an extra precaution, I used the manacles to secure him to the floor.

"I watched Ara when she was with you." His thick accent almost caused me to miss Brea's alias. "If I had a woman like that, I would not turn her over to the authorities."

Already at the door, I turned and scowled. "It's none of your concern."

"In San Tesoro, we know the value of having a good woman by your side."

This wasn't meant to be personal, but I suddenly felt a powerful urge to defend myself and my intentions toward Brea. However I squelched that impulse and used this to further the cover story. "You met her yesterday, and you think you know her?"

He lifted his chin. "I watched her face when she first saw you. Before she was angry and afraid, she wore the face of a woman whose heart has been broken. She does not hide her emotions well."

I was in a position to know that Brea could—and did—hide her emotions very well. Not only that, she was great at faking it. This man, at least, had bought her entire act. I pressed my lips together and exhaled. "If it'll make you feel better, returning her to the US isn't part of my plan. She's beautiful, strong, and stubborn. Sometimes a woman needs a man to show her that he's stronger and more stubborn."

The guard's frown turned from righteous indignation to understanding and acceptance. I'd appealed to his machismo, and it had worked.

"I'd untie you, but I can't take the chance that you'll interfere with my mission." I closed the door and secured the locks. Returning to

Jesse, I found him hooked up to another port a few rows down in the server room. "How's it coming?"

"Good. I ran a search for Cuyler, and I came up with interesting stuff."

"That's probably why he wanted the servers destroyed."

"The CIA is at odds with the current administration. Rocha has evidence that they're running unsanctioned clandestine operations counter to policy and direct orders." Jesse swiped and tapped at the information on the screen. "The stuff on the Senate might take down a few officials, but the people behind the scenes, the ones really running the show, won't be impacted." He disconnected his device and inserted a small card into a slot in one of the server's components.

"What's that?"

"A virus that'll leave holes in data files." His gaze swept the room. "Rocha's good, though, so this won't be more than a short-term pain in his ass. I admire the guy's setup. If you're going to be an info-terrorist, this is the way to do it."

"Are you done?"

"Almost. I just have to double check whether the virus works. I didn't have a chance to perfect it before we left." He went to a terminal and tapped out commands on the keyboard. Using his own device would only lead to this operation backfiring when the virus infected Jesse's tech.

While he did that, I rooted around in the drawers. I wasn't looking for anything specific, but I found our comms. I inserted mine into my ear and handed one to Jesse. We checked to make sure they worked, and then I took one out to Frankie.

I found her strolling along the deck and caressing the semi-automatic she'd liberated from our captors. I held out the earpiece. "Look what I found."

"Wonderful. When do you think Ara and Isa are coming back?" She motioned to the mountain surrounding the house on three sides. "If they're looking for buried treasure, there's a lot of ground to cover, and I would be surprised if this area wasn't riddled with caves. It's mostly limestone."

I had no idea. "She expects us to do our thing and head for the hills."

"But we're not." Frankie drummed her fingertips on the railing. "We don't leave a man behind, even if that man is two women who don't follow our plan."

"Getting captured wasn't part of our plan."

"You know how we're turning away jobs and recommending them to other firms?" She turned to me. "Don't you think we'd be better served by bringing Brea and Jessica on board as full members of the team? A con artist and a CIA operative have a lot of the same training."

None of us had CIA or FBI training. We were great with stealthy operations that required surgical precision, but we weren't spies. We weren't well-versed in infiltration. The undercover work I'd done at my father's firm had utilized the extent of our experience in that arena. I knew that Frankie's suggestion was in the best interest for the growth of our firm.

Still I doubted Brea would take the job. She'd made it clear that she wanted to be a treasure hunter. The only reason she'd agreed to work part-time as our manager was because Jesse had begged her to come back.

Frankie wrinkled her nose. "Something to consider."

Jesse joined us on the deck, and together we watched the sun set over the trees.

Brea: Some Treasures are Worth More Than Others

"Isa, Juan will carry you on his back." Carvalho made this decree as he stopped yet again to wait for us to catch up. "How do you expect to hunt for treasure when you cannot bear a strenuous hike?"

Jessica grimaced. "I've been doing well, and it's not like we have much of a choice."

Juan crouched down and helped Jessica onto his back. I took her cane. She wrapped her arms around his neck and rested her head against his shoulder, utterly exhausted.

Carvalho snorted. "It seems to me that the Bella Sisters who were able to take down my father could have come up with a better scheme."

"It's not a scheme." I defended us. "We left that life behind."

"Not far enough behind. It followed you to San Tesoro. It's waiting for you in my dungeon." He chuckled. "Tell me, Ara. How did you come to be involved with a bounty hunter?"

When spinning a lie, it was best to stick as close to the truth as possible, and since I'd already told him this story, I needed to make sure my story was consistent. "A friend introduced us. I thought I was going to Top him, and he wanted someone to be his sub."

Since I walked next to him now, Carvalho glanced over. The lift of his brows was barely discernible in the small amount of light reflecting back to us from our flashlights. "It looks like you won."

"Yes." I grinned smugly, and I let the grin fade to melancholy. "And no. I think about the look on his face when he found out that I'm not who he thought I was, and it cuts me. He felt betrayed. I never wanted that."

"Did you know who he was?"

I shook my head, channeling the heartbreak that had come when I'd found out David had been investigating me when we'd first met. "He was this handsome, charming guy with a cute smile and a great sense of humor. I really, really liked him, and then it turned out he was a jerk." I shook my head as if to get rid of the negative memory. "I'm never going to meet a man like that again, and after this experience, I certainly don't want to."

"Have you thought about what you'll do if you don't find a treasure?"

Heaving a sigh, I stabbed the ground with the tip of Jessica's cane. "Finding an actual treasure is a long shot. When you get to the point where a long shot is all you have left, you find yourself considering unappealing options."

"Such as stealing from a handsome, wealthy, former lover?"

I knew that's where he'd take my comment, but I laughed as if that's the last thing I'd considered. "I've already done that. The money you found is what I took from David. He had it in his apartment. Bounty hunters never know when they're going to need a pile of cash."

He sidled a look at me, or so I thought that's what he did. It was too dark to tell. "Have you considered that's the reason he's pursuing you?"

For a long time I didn't answer. I wanted him to think I was considering his question. When I did respond, I spoke softly. "He kissed me back."

Thoroughly exhausted, we walked most of the rest of the way in silence. When the bright lights of the house came into view, I breathed a sigh of relief. We emerged from the woods to find that telltale red light from a laser site focused on our chests. My heart beat faster. As I watched, the red dots moved to center on Carvalho, Juan, Jose, and Diego.

We stopped short, looking for the source of the threat, and bright flashlights blinded us.

"Ara, Isa—come here." David's authoritative tone made my heart race for a different reason. He was supposed to be long gone.

I looked to Carvalho. He motioned to Juan. "Put her down. Let the ladies go with these fine bounty hunters."

Stunned, I turned to Carvalho. "What?"

"Sorry, darling, but you've become a liability."

Juan set Jessica on her feet, taking a moment to steady her. She took a step toward me.

"Wait." Carvalho held up a hand. "Juan, please relieve the lovely Isa of her burden."

Now I understood his game. I whirled on him, pointing an accusatory finger. "You want the treasure for yourself."

He didn't bother to hide his hungry grin. "When you first came, I thought the whole treasure thing was bullshit. But given what we've found, I think there is actual merit to your story."

"And your story makes sense." Diego stepped forward to take Jessica's backpack. "My people were enslaved by the Spanish long ago. There are tales of hidden silver mines in this area. With your map, we'll find them, and Cadez will become a tourist destination."

I looked between them. "You cooked this up at the stream."

Carvalho stuck his hands in his pockets and affected a boyish smile. "Maybe you will get your wish and your bounty hunter will sweep you off your feet instead of sending you to prison?"

I knew this was a scam—finding that morion had been a stroke of luck—but a vital part of me had enjoyed the hunt for buried treasure. Without pausing to consider the ramifications of my actions, I aimed a punch squarely at Carvalho's nose. Cartilage crunched, and blood gushed down his face.

An arm wrapped around my waist, and I found myself lifted and carried. Diego set me in front of David. "You will make sure neither woman returns here."

David handed Diego a zip tie and took the cane from me. "I don't want her taking a swing at me. She hates me more than she hates him."

Diego tied my wrists, and I glared at David. "I can't believe you're having him do your dirty work."

Jesse and Frankie came forward, emerging from shadows so dark I hadn't seen them. I'd wondered if they'd left David here so that they could get the information out of the country, but my gut told me that they wouldn't leave without us even though I'd told David to go. They patted down our captors, removing guns and knives from each man. Juan, Jose, Diego, and Carvalho willingly got on their knees and let themselves be tied up.

"You understand," Jesse said. "We can't just leave you free."

"Of course." Carvalho said. "I would do the same thing in your position."

Just because Carvalho was being a jerk, I chimed in. "There is a knife in the bag full of cooking supplies."

Frankie wouldn't meet my eyes, but she got to work collecting all the bags—including the one Jessica had been carrying.

Jose glared at me.

I stuck out my tongue. "Serves you right. I hope a scorpion and a brown recluse have a sword fight on your butt and a poison tree frog licks your left cheek."

Jessica took a step toward me, probably to cut me off before I got on a roll, and she stumbled. Jesse scooped her up in his arms. "Let's go. There's a flight out in an hour."

The five of us followed the path to the garage. David poked the nose of his gun into my lower back to keep up appearances. I hoped the safety was on.

"How come you're not tying her up? She's a fugitive from justice every bit as much as I am." I went for maximum irritation and volume.

David pressed the button on a key fob he'd taken, probably from the house. The lights on a black SUV flashed. He cut the ties binding my wrists. "Get in the car, Sugar." His low tenor teased my senses, calming me immediately.

Frankie took the driver's seat, and Jesse rode shotgun. Literally, he held two big, assault-style weapons that he pointed out the window. Jesse had put Jessica into the car first, so I slid into the middle and let David sit next to me. With the doors closed and nothing but the breeze coming through Jesse's open window, I relaxed.

Jessica closed her eyes and leaned against my shoulder. "I'm going to sleep for a week."

I patted her cheek. "We did it. We were freaking awesome."

On the other side of me, David cleared his throat. I turned, ready for him to ream me out for what we'd done. "Allergies?"

"Crow."

"What?"

"You were right. Infiltration worked. We're leaving with everything we came to get, and Rocha is under the impression we're doing him a favor." He twined his fingers in mine.

"You helped him steal treasure from us."

He chuckled. "You actually sound upset."

"We had maps and a diary." Perhaps Jessica had fabricated them, but her information had been based on actual research, and we'd found an artifact at one of the locations.

"Really?"

I leaned forward. "Frankie, you kept Jessica's backpack, right?"

She kept her eyes on the road as she spoke. "Yes, but the one guy took out some papers. I figured it was best to let him have what he wanted. Otherwise we risk them coming after us."

"You don't think they'll come for the car?"

Jesse chimed in. "We'll leave it nearby with the keys under the seat."

Just then, Frankie slowed and pulled over. "There's our vehicle. Let's get out of here."

"Our suitcase is at Carvalho's." Three sour expressions had me backpedaling. "Fine. I'm used to leaving my things behind."

Jesse helped Jessica into the car they'd procured, handling her as if she was porcelain. Nobody seemed surprised by this development, but I couldn't stop stress from tightening in my gut. I loved my sister unconditionally, but I loved Jesse too. I grieved for the heart she was about to break.

David and Frankie ignored me as they did military stuff where they looked around to make sure nobody was going to jump out of the bushes and murder us before we could pull off a spectacular and star-studded getaway.

Sandwiched between Jessica and David once again, I remained silent until the bright lights of Abundante came into view. We weren't far from the airport. Jessica's eyes fluttered open, and she sat up, disoriented from running on too little sleep.

"It's a good thing I have our passports in my bag since you wouldn't go back for our suitcase."

David stared at me. "I guess that means we don't have to leave you here after all."

Jessica chuckled, her normal effervescence subverted into a quiet amusement. "She also has about five thousand dollars in cash in there."

David gasped. "You brought *all* the cash I gave you?"

Jesse twisted around in his seat. "They could sell it to Customs as vacation cash. I'm sure there's a good reason to be wary of traveler's checks."

Jessica and I responded at the same time. "Cash is accepted everywhere and doesn't leave a paper trail."

With an amused laugh, David said, "I should have known."

Before we left, Jessica and I disappeared into the bathroom to clean up the morion and make it look like a souvenir.

Even though our flight arrived in the pre-dawn hours, Dean met us at the airport. He'd traded in his usual jacket-and-tie for a purple sweater vest over a lavender shirt with gray slacks. A pair of expensive sunglasses hung from the V of his vest, and he'd recently trimmed his hair.

I stopped in front of him and looked him up and down. "Damn, you look like you spent the past few days at a spa."

"Yeah," Jesse's dry tone sucked moisture from the vicinity. "You're really rocking those soft pastels. It distracts from your beefcake persona."

Jessica leaned heavily on her cane. "You got laid. I can tell from the sparkle in your eyes."

"Remind me to tell you about it later." He winked at Jessica before taking a closer look at Jesse, Frankie, and David. Though he didn't comment, I knew he was cataloging their various injuries. "I take it Brea and Jessica decided on a Central American vacation?"

"Yes." Frankie stepped to the front of the pack. "They were freaking awesome. We wouldn't have made it home without them. How about you take us home so we can shower, rest, and debrief?"

"Debrief first. Someone is going to want his data." He held his arm out to Jessica. "How's the leg?"

She threaded her arm through his. "I've had better days."

He held his other arm out to Frankie, but she declined, a gentle scowl marring her chin.

Jesse, jaw set hard, took a step forward. I knew he wanted to be the one who helped Jessica, but if he made a scene now, she would publicly reject him. Maybe he could withstand that, but I couldn't. I put a hand on his biceps. "Be patient. I'll suggest he drop her at your apartment so that you can drive her home, okay?"

He glanced away. "Her place is on the way." It was likely that Jessica would be the first one dropped off.

David slung his arm around my waist, but I maintained hold of Jesse's arm until we got to the car. As I got inside, David whispered in my ear, "Sugar, I aim to have us married sooner rather than later."

"I hope you all slept on the plane." Dean cut off two sleepy, early-morning drivers and sped from the parking lot. "It's necessary to have you all there for the debrief."

I wanted to protest. Though I'd slept on the plane, I was still very tired, and both Jessica and I were still grimy from our long trek through a San Tesoro jungle. I glanced at David and saw that he was resigned to Dean's plan, and I tabled my objection for all of ten minutes. I felt gross, and I'm sure I was at least part of the reason Frankie opted to have her window rolled down. As Dean exited the freeway, I leaned closer to David. "I'm going to shower when we get there."

He nodded. "You are a bit ripe."

Wedged into the smaller third row seat—Dean hadn't expected to pick five people up from the airport, or else he would have brought a larger vehicle—Jesse laughed. "Sounds like you forgot how to sweet talk your lady. Even after an airport bath, I think we're all a bit ripe."

Jessica and I followed everybody to the top floor. While they went into the conference room, I led her to the locker room on the third floor. "I have extra clothes here that'll fit you." Since Frankie had started making me work out regularly, I'd begun keeping some workout clothes in my locker. After we showered, I came up short in the shirt department, so I took one from David's locker even though Frankie's shirt would have fit me much better. And she also had an extra sports bra in there, which I stopped Jessica from borrowing.

"You can't take things without permission." I put Frankie's bra back in her locker. "It's one of their rules."

Jessica rolled her eyes and donned my shirt. "If Jesse spends the whole meeting staring at my headlights, I will smack him."

I wanted to reassure her, but where Jesse was concerned, I wasn't certain he'd keep his gaze pointed at her face. "Let's get up there. They're going to want to hear our side of the story."

In the elevator, which we took because Jessica was still unsteady on her feet and tired from yesterday's exertion, she pouted. "We don't have to tell them anything."

From the corner of my eye, I gave her a long look. "We have nothing to hide."

During the meeting, she left me to do all the talking. David, Jesse, and Frankie took us through how Rocha's men got the drop on them, and I related how we snared Carvalho's interest and let him screw us over.

"Bait and switch." Frankie smirked. "I like it. David and I were talking before you and Jessica returned to Rocha's mansion. Being trained for various special forces, we envisioned SAFE Security as a company that helped people with very specific types of problems. Over the years, we've turned down jobs like this because they've required skills we don't have."

I stared, both waiting for her to continue and for my brain to figure out a context. When she said nothing, I looked to David and Jessica. David smiled, and Jessica shrugged. "Are we finished with the briefing?"

"Not yet." Jesse cleared his throat. "Brea and Jessica, you both have skills that are useful for infiltration, the kinds of missions the CIA or a con artist might run. We've come to realize that you both have a lot to offer a firm like SAFE Security."

"I smell a job offer." Jessica spoke for the first time since we'd been there. "And not the kind that involves answering phones."

"Yes," David said. "We'd like for the both of you to join the team."

As I had suggested this over a year ago, I waited for someone to deliver the punch line.

Jessica frowned. "SAFEZZ Security doesn't have the same ring to it."

Jesse laughed, but neither Frankie nor Dean found it funny. David said, "We're not changing the name of the company. Besides, Brea is going to be an Eastridge very soon."

"SAFEEZ isn't much better." Jessica snorted and pushed her chair back. "I'm not interested."

I gaped at her. "Yes, you are. We had a blast in San Tesoro. We're good at this, Jessica."

She struggled to her feet. "If anything, this has taught me that I'm not ready for field work."

"Planning," Jesse said. "Missions that don't require strenuous physical activity. Don't turn this down because you're afraid of me."

She scowled. "I'm not afraid of you."

Before things could escalate, the chime sounded to indicate someone had entered the elevator that would bring them to the fourth floor. Dean and David rose, armed themselves, and went to greet our visitor.

I looked to Frankie. "Grayson Cuyler?"

"Probably." She didn't seem concerned, but that wasn't a measure of the amount of danger coming our way.

"He's going to want what he sent us to get." Jesse got to his feet. "I'll be right back."

Once they were all gone, I faced Frankie. "Whose idea was it to make us members of your team?"

"I suggested it, but David was the one who pushed for it today. He's come a long way, Brea, thanks to you." A small smile curved her lips. "It's okay to say yes. We really do want both of you here full time. Plus it's safer if we know about the cases you take."

I winced at the dig alluding to the case I'd taken that had resulted in the deaths of six men who'd tried to storm this very building. "Yeah. Maybe. Probably. I mean, I pretty much am already, right?"

"You're going to need a new office manager." Jessica fiddled with a paper clip. "Not me, though. I'm going to devote my time to treasure hunting and running Unexpected Treasures."

The door opened, and David ushered Grayson Cuyler inside. Dean and Jesse followed. Grayson's gaze roved the room, taking in Jessica, Frankie, and me. Dressed in a polo shirt and slacks, he didn't look at all like a government spook.

"I see you're all safe as houses." He flashed a million-dollar smile. "I'll just get my item and be on my way."

"Not so fast." Dean closed the door. "Have a seat."

Before Grayson could decline, David pulled out a chair. "That wasn't Dean being polite."

I grinned. "I'm not going to offer you a cupcake or coffee, either."

Jessica slowly resumed her seat.

Grayson threw his hands up in a gesture of surrender and sat down, that grin never fading from his lips. "This is where you tell me that you've had enough, and you never want to see me again. I'm not feeling the love, people."

David and Dean positioned themselves near the door, and Jesse took a seat across from Grayson. Jesse gently placed an SD card on the table, which is where Grayson's attention went. At least it did until Dean threw a file folder down in front of him.

Grayson opened the folder. I appreciated how he didn't hem and haw. He dove right into the mystery. He flipped pages, looking at images and reading things. I had no idea as to the content of this ambush, but I enjoyed watching him wiggle.

At last he closed the folder and met David's gaze. "So?"

Tightly controlled fury gleamed in David's eyes. "That information makes you look like a domestic terrorist. The CIA or NEO or whatever agency you're working for isn't allowed to carry out operations against US citizens."

Again, Grayson shrugged.

Dean added, "Insinuating yourself into the operation of a small organized crime unit in the heartland of the country isn't CIA business."

"You're right. It's FBI business." Grayson's feathers remained unruffled.

"You're not in the FBI." I lifted a brow, challenging him. "And you're not in the CIA. You don't work for the government at all. Nothing you've done is sanctioned."

He leaned forward. "You're thinking my threat to throw you and Jessica into a deep hole at a black site is hollow? I assure you that it's not. Would you care for a demonstration?"

"Cut the bullshit," Jessica said. "We're calling your bluff. If you don't leave us alone, then we're going public with everything. Do you honestly think the US government is going to stand by you? You're expendable."

By way of response, he smiled. "I knew I liked you the best. Beautiful, smart, with ovaries of steel. If you get tired of hanging around this place, give me a call."

Jesse got up and came around the table to stand over Grayson. He didn't bother to temper his threatening manner, and the smile on Grayson's face finally vanished. "Rocha collected a lot of information on a lot of people. Before I infected his computer with a virus, I ran a complex search, and I hit pay dirt on you. Venezuela, Kazakhstan, Aleppo—sanctioned or unsanctioned, the things for which you're responsible will end your career. We're finished with you, Cuyler. You are no longer welcome here."

Grayson pressed his lips together briefly. "Before you burn this bridge, you might look at what happened to the firm you subcontracted with for that job David and Jesse were supposed to go on. What was it? Fournier Security?"

Dean's glance sidled to David. "A truck carrying fertilizer overturned and exploded, killing the men who went on that mission in your places. It wasn't an accident."

The loudest silence overtook the room. My ears buzzed at the idea that I might have lost David.

"You knew that op was going to go sideways. You killed them." Frankie's quiet statement broke into the whirlwind of my thoughts. "You can't expect us to believe you did all this just to keep David and Jesse away from there."

"Of course not." Grayson's trademark smile resurfaced. "You took care of Rocha for me."

"It wasn't coincidence," David said.

Grayson shrugged. "I would never misuse sensitive intel." He got to his feet and snagged the SD card. "You know, most ex-military people with your skills end up dealing arms, running drugs, or something equally unsavory. Very few make it their business to have a positive impact on those who are mostly innocent. I like what you're doing with your life." He headed to the door and waited while David and Dean moved out of his way.

Once he was gone, I went to David and slipped my arms around his waist. "I'm kind of glad he did what he did."

David returned my embrace. "He could have just asked me not to go."

"He probably couldn't. You know—top secret and all that kind of crap." Actually he'd approached first with an offer. Threats and blackmail came later. I lifted my face so that I could look into his eyes. "He's got to be CIA or NEO"

"I know. We were just rattling his cage to see what shook out." He pressed a kiss to my forehead. "Let's go home and get some sleep. The rest of this will keep until tomorrow."

I motioned behind me to where Jessica waited. "Let's take Jessica home first."

"Anything for you, Sugar."

Jesse stepped closer to Jessica. "I'll take her home."

Jessica opened her mouth to say something, but she closed it without speaking, and she followed Jesse from the room. I fervently hoped she would be kind to him.

Eleven days later I found myself in the bathroom of my parents' new home outside of KC. Hanging on the back of the door was the bold green dress I'd selected. It had simple, elegant lines, and the color brought out my eyes without competing with them. I stared at it as I sat on a stool wearing a robe with only a bra and panties underneath.

Sylvia unrolled my hair from around a thick curler while Jessica fussed with my eyelashes.

"I wish you'd wear your hair up," Sylvia said. "I can do a coif that would complement the elegance of your dress."

"I don't want the scars on my neck to show. The dress has a square neckline, so my hair has to cover up my neck and shoulder." When David had said he wanted to get married as soon as possible, I hadn't realized his timeline would be so short. By the time I had rolled out of bed the afternoon after our adventure, David had everything set up—location, flowers, catering, and officiant. All I had to do was to select a dress and ask Jessica to be my maid of honor.

"David doesn't notice them." Sylvia scoffed, but the hands working on my hairstyle remained gentle. "He likes when you wear your hair away from your face."

Jessica giggled, and then she mocked me. "For some reason, he thinks you're pretty. Even after seeing what you look like first thing in the morning, he still wants to marry you."

David had taken over Jessica's apartment behind the garage so the groomsmen could get ready, which left us the rest of the house. I imagined Dean was helping him dress while Jesse provided the teasing designed to settle his nerves.

"I don't know why he's in such a hurry. It's not like I knocked him up or anything."

"Am I going to be a grandmother?" Sylvia sounded entirely too pleased and not at all surprised.

My hair jerked from her hold as I twisted around to look up at her. "Hell, no. This is not a shotgun wedding."

She lifted her chin toward the trash under the sink. "When I emptied the trash earlier, I found an early pregnancy test in there. I couldn't help but notice that it's positive."

I drew back. "Well it isn't mine."

There weren't all that many people here. On my side, I'd invited my parents, my sister, and my brother. Julianne had flown here from Michigan even though I'd been a crappy friend since we'd moved away. Neither my siblings nor Julianne had brought a date. The only other woman here was Frankie, and I couldn't see her taking a pregnancy test at someone else's house. She was a very private person. I wasn't sure about Julianne, but somehow I didn't think it was hers.

Slowly I turned to Jessica. I said nothing, but she didn't meet my gaze, and that's when I knew. She picked up a brush and set to work on my cheekbones. "Please don't say a word to anyone. I haven't decided what I'm going to do."

"Sure. Whatever you want. I'm here for you." I spoke softly, remembering the last time Jessica had been pregnant. We'd just broken away from BS, and she'd had an abortion. But things were different now. She had a steady job, a place to live, and support from more than just me.

Sylvia rested a hand on Jessica's shoulder. "I'm here for you too, sweetheart."

Tears welled in Jessica's eyes, but she willed them away. "Thank you, but please don't tell anyone, not Dad and especially not David, okay?" Before I could say anything, she dried her cheeks and resumed doing my makeup. "This is your day. You only get one first wedding."

I clicked my tongue at her attempted joke. "This is it for me. 'Til death and all that."

We let that topic slide away as they beautified me so that I could change my name for the final time. Moments seemed to both blur and go in slow motion. Before I knew it, a recording of The Wedding March was playing and I found myself staring down a length of white fabric strewn with rose petals. Dean stood at the far end, a leatherbound volume in one hand. Next to him stood the man of my dreams, looking incredibly handsome and fairly jittery in his black tuxedo and emerald green cummerbund.

Frankie and Leon sat on one side of the aisle, and Sylvia sat on the other side between Julianne and an empty chair.

Warren—my real father—tucked my hand under his arm. He leaned down and kissed my temple. "If you change your mind, my car is gassed up and ready to go."

Surprised that he'd offer that option, I gaped at him. "I thought you liked David?"

His green eyes, identical to my own, sparkled with pride and deeper emotions. "I do, but you're my daughter. I love you. Nothing is more important than your happiness, angel."

I hugged him. "I love you too, and I want to marry him."

The ceremony, like the day, happened in stop motion—a series of pictures that no photographer could capture. I memorized the way love radiated from David's core, the arrogant slant to his lips as he pledged his heart and fidelity to me, and the possessive gleam in his light brown eyes when I said my vows. The heat and strength of his hand as it held mine ingrained itself in the deepest recesses of my soul. By the time he slipped the ring on my finger and kissed me to seal the deal, I shook with the force of overwhelming emotion, and so he held me to him until the quaking subsided.

Before I could make a return trip down the short aisle, I found myself engulfed by a hug from Dean. "Welcome to the family, Sugar."

Jessica, being the next closest to me, handed me back my bouquet and hugged me next. "Congratulations, little sister."

I turned, and found myself in Jesse's arms. He kissed my cheek. "Now you're never getting rid of us, Sugar."

While I was being hugged to death, David was also accepting congratulatory hugs and handshakes. I heard Warren tell David to take good care of me, and Sylvia cried as she hugged him.

I faced Julianne, the woman who'd been a good friend to me when I'd been alone in the world. It had been months since I'd called or texted, and I felt guilty about it. "Hey. It's good to see you."

"Yeah." She glanced away, and I realized that she probably felt guilty as well. "I've been busy with my mom and stuff." Her mother had been battling one health problem after another, and Julianne had been her primary caregiver. "Thanks for inviting me."

I hugged her, and not just to stop the awkward conversation. I'd missed her terribly, and I hadn't realized it until seeing her just now. "We aren't going on a honeymoon just yet. Are you going to stick around for a few days?"

"Sure. Summer—Jessica—invited me to stay with her."

David inserted himself into the conversation. He hugged Julianne. "Thanks for flying out on such short notice. Brea would love to go out for a late lunch with you tomorrow."

My brows lifted. "A late lunch?"

His grin turned devilish. "I plan to exhaust you tonight."

The crowd laughed, and my face flushed with heat because I knew he meant it. Later that night, we slow danced together in our apartment. His hands roamed over my hips and ass while his mouth captured mine. The kiss seared my senses. He drugged me with his nearness and the heat of his body against mine. I almost didn't hear him when he asked me a question.

"Are you ready for your first scene as a married woman?"

We'd discussed this at length since our return home. I nodded, my lips so close to his that they brushed an accidental kiss against his. "Yes. Are you?"

He laughed, the nervous kind of a man who has accepted his fate. "I'm ready, my Sugar Queen."

"Go and change. I'll get things set up out here."

He'd already moved the dining table out of the way. A lone chair waited in the center of the dining room—the one we'd bought at the flea market. Jessica had cleaned it up and glued it together for this occasion. I retrieved the bag I'd placed on the table earlier. It contained the equipment he'd approved, including handcuffs, a ball gag, and the cock ring that I used to rock his world. Then I quick-changed into a short skirt and a shirt with a low neckline.

A quarter hour later, he emerged from the bedroom. The tuxedo was gone, replaced by an old T-shirt and cargo pants. Both were ripped and worse for wear after having barely survived his trip to San Tesoro. The tears showed off his well-muscled body, and I couldn't help but take a moment to admire the sexy man who was now my husband.

I picked up the riding crop, crossed the room, and held it against his chest like it was a cattle prod. "It is time for your interrogation, prisoner. Sit." Using the crop, I guided him to the chair where he sat down. He cooperated while I handcuffed his wrists behind his back and to the slats on the back of the chair.

"I won't answer your questions," he warned with a dangerous slant to his mouth as I tied his ankles to the legs of the chair with rope.

Dragging the flap of the crop from the top of his sternum down to his navel, I chuckled. He ignored the crop and kept his powerful gaze on mine. I loomed over him and used the crop to force him to tilt his face upward. This made him appear submissive even if he wasn't feeling it yet.

"You'll be surprised at the things I'm going to make you do."

"You can't make me do anything."

I lifted one corner of my mouth in a sinister grin, and I retrieved the scissors. These shears were new and very sharp. I dragged the tip along his shoulder and across his chest. He couldn't hide the way his pulse kicked up a notch or the nervous swallow made his Adam's apple bob. Teasing him—or terrorizing him—a little more, I slid the edge of the scissors down his thighs, and then I made a return trip. I did this a second time, and then I opened the scissors. He watched, uncertain, as I pulled the collar of his shirt away from his skin, and the cold metal of the scissors came into contact with his skin.

Slowly I cut away his clothes, taking breaks to slide the shears across his skin and get his breathing going even faster. I hadn't meant for this to be a sensual experience, but it appeared I'd discovered something my Dominant submissive hadn't known he liked. I finished baring him, and I looked up to find his eyes closed and his lips parted. I watched him for a moment, soaking in his enjoyment of my Domination.

While he was lost in bliss, I slid the cock ring down his semi-hard dick. Then I wrapped my hand around his cock. "This belongs to me."

David opened his eyes and looked down at me.

"Say it," I ordered as I worked it with my hand. "Say that this dick belongs to your Sugar Queen."

"Never." Even though he refused, his cock hardened under my deft touch. "It's mine."

I closed my mouth around his cock, cradling it with my tongue, and it finished lengthening. I sucked him harder and to a faster rhythm, and then I pulled back to run the tip of my tongue along the sensitive crown of his cock. He moaned and lifted his hips, and that's when I drew away.

"Say this cock is mine. Beg me to fuck you." I scratched his inner thighs lightly, and he moaned.

"No. Never. You'll never win this."

I didn't argue the point. Instead I waged war. I ran my palms over his body, touching his stomach, legs, shoulders, and arms. Straddling him, I caressed his face and nibbled on his earlobe. Then I reached between our bodies and fisted the silky softness of the cock in question. "This is mine, all mine." I kissed him lightly, playing my lips across his and feathering soft bites along the edges of his mouth.

He tried to capture my lips for a deeper kiss, and so I leaned away and stood over him. I lifted the hem of my skirt and showed him that I wore nothing underneath. His gaze riveted there, and I felt myself growing hotter and wetter even though he was only looking at me. With two fingers, I spread my pussy lips. Using my other hand, I circled my clit. It felt good, and I rocked my hips forward, opening myself even more.

"You want this," I cooed.

"I'm going to get out of these restraints." His molten gaze promised pleasure and retribution. "And then I'm going to tie you up and fuck you until I've had enough."

I backed away from him, not because I was retreating, but because I wasn't finished breaking him to my will. Running my hands up my body, I lifted my shirt over my head, revealing a white strapless bra. Through the lacy fabric, I took each breast in hand, kneading while he watched.

"Clamps," he said. "I'm going to suck those tits until you scream, and then I'm going to put clamps on your nipples. I'll thread a chain through them, and as I fuck you, I'll pull on it to torture those luscious breasts."

He may have been bucking for top dog, but according to the rules of our game, I could do to him anything he threatened to do to me. I recognized the moment he realized his mistake. It didn't take but a minute to retrieve the nipple clamps from the bedroom.

"This is going to hurt, my thief, and I will enjoy your suffering." I worked his nipple, pinching it softly and working up to hard and cruel. He cried out a protest when I tightened down the clamp—I hadn't gone for the clover his first time around—and I waited for him to call yellow. When he didn't, I caressed his cheek with the backs of my knuckles. "It's not so bad, is it?"

He gritted his teeth.

"Are you ready to admit this cock belongs to me and that I'm your Queen?"

He shook his head once, and determination hardened his chocolate eyes.

I wasn't so gentle with his remaining nipple. He shouted and bucked, moving the chair several inches. When he calmed, I connected them with a delicate chain. Glancing down, I noted that David's hard-on had not diminished. If anything, it throbbed harder. I regarded him with a gentle smile. "It seems you're a bit of a masochist."

By way of reply, he grunted.

I removed my skirt. Now all I wore was a white lace strapless bra and the silk stockings in which I'd been married. David's hungry gaze raked my body from head to toe. I licked my finger and touched my clit.

"Bring that pretty pussy here. I'll show you something better."

"Ask nicely," I admonished. "Beg."

He pressed his lips together, but only for second. "Please," he said, but he used the tone that meant he'd given an order.

One of the fun things I'd put in my bag of tricks was a vibrating wand. I took it out and powered it up. I straddled David, standing over him with my legs spread, and I pressed the head of the wand to my clit.

Watching me masturbate always drove David crazy. He pitched forward, and I felt his mouth move along my midsection, laving a hot, wet path of pleasure. I wanted to stay where I was, but I couldn't let him have the upper hand, so I backed away. It placed a throw pillow on the floor and knelt down in front of him. Then I set the vibrator against the sensitive underside of his cock. I traced it down his length and massaged his balls. He moaned, groaned, and swore.

"My cock," I said as I licked it from ring to tip. "All mine."

"Yes," he breathed on the wings of a sigh. "Yours. This cock is yours, my Sugar Queen."

I rewarded him with a kiss, and then I sank down on the cock that belonged to me. I rocked and rotated, fucking him with abandon. Sounds of pleasure came from him as he submitted to me. I pulled on the chain connecting the clamps as I rode, and he cried out at the pleasure-pain combination. Sensations build in my core, a sweet heat that washed over me in waves of orgasmic bliss.

I lost the rhythm, but I was beyond caring. I collapsed forward and rested my head against his shoulder. His hard cock was still inside me, prolonging the pulsing of my climax. Before I knew what was happening, I found myself lifted. I jerked from my post-climax stupor and tried to wrest from his hold. "How did you get free?"

He threw me over his shoulder. "Paperclip. I didn't drop it this time."

"I didn't give you a paperclip," I sputtered. "You weren't supposed to get free."

"Always search a prisoner, Sugar." He slapped my ass. "Especially when he's a reluctant sub."

"But you suck with picking locks! I'm not buying that you used a paperclip. You got the backup key and cheated."

"Nope. Sorry, Sugar. I've been practicing with Dean."

He carried me to the bedroom and threw me on the bed. Then he stood over me, silently daring me to try to escape. I noticed he still wore the nipple clamps. He noticed as well. He hissed as he removed the first one, and he swore when he got to the second one.

While he was occupied, I scrambled off the bed. I didn't know where I planned to go, but our rules clearly stated that once he was untied, he was no longer under my control.

He caught me around the waist and lifted me off my feet.

I kicked wildly. "How did you get your feet free?"

"You suck at tying knots." He set me on the bed, belly down, and straddled me. This position effectively immobilized me. The clasp of my bra loosened, and the scrap of fabric fell away. He positioned my arm behind my back, and I felt the familiar slide of silk rope across my skin. "I'll show you what real ropework looks like, Sugar."

Without much cooperation from me, he bound my arms behind my back. We were both careful with my left shoulder, and he didn't tie me tight enough to force my shoulders back. Then he flipped me over—still straddling me—and tied the remaining rope so that it framed my breasts. We both knew I wouldn't be able to stay this way for long, but I could tell that David planned to make the most of it.

He shimmied down my body, trapping my legs between his powerful thighs, and his mouth fastened on my nipple. As he'd threatened, he sucked hard. I cried out—in protest and in pleasure—but he didn't stop until he felt like it. That's when he clipped those very same clamps onto my swollen nipples. I breathed against the sudden and sharp pain, waiting for it to morph into something tingly and pleasurable.

While I was busy doing that, he lifted my legs, pushing them up and open. He leaned over me, and his thick cock penetrated my tissues. He pumped into me, his pace frenetic. The tendons on his neck stood out as he concentrated. Another orgasm overtook me, but the cock ring prevented him from coming. The tide may have turned, but my little toy still ruled the night.

"Son of a bitch." He pulled out and flipped me over so that my ass was in the air and my face was in the covers. He thrust into me, harder and faster, smacking my ass to a different rhythm. Then I felt his hand in my hair, pulling my head up and back. The move caused the chain to catch on the rumpled bedclothes. The combination of sensations pushed me over the edge yet again. Without the covers to muffle it, I'm sure our neighbor heard my scream.

"Fuck, Sugar. You feel so good. So hot. So freaking amazing." He kept up the pace while I floated. I wasn't sure how much time passed before he was able to climax, but I felt hot jets of semen bathing my insides as he cried out every bit as loudly as I had. He collapsed, rolling so that he didn't put pressure on my bonds and hurt my shoulder.

I watched his chest rise and fall as he panted and enjoyed the aftermath of his orgasm. I wished my arms were free so that I could hold him. "Are you going to untie me now?"

"How's your shoulder?"

"Getting sore. But mostly I want to snuggle with you."

With a few strategic pulls, he freed my arms without completely untying me. I scooted so that I was nestled in the crook of his arm. He rolled toward me and enveloped me in his embrace. "Wife, this switching thing isn't half bad."

"You cheated," I said.

"Hmmm." He smiled, and I felt it against my head. "I learned from the best."

SAFE SECURITY

Dear Reader,

I hope you enjoyed reading about David and Brea as much as I love writing about them. These characters are close to my heart, and I hope they've winnowed their way into yours as well.

Their adventures and their love story are only just beginning. Stay in touch. Let me know your thoughts. Email and social media are great, but your reviews and recommendations help other readers find my books. They make a difference—even if they're just a few heartfelt words. Please consider leaving an honest review on Amazon, Goodreads, iTunes, Barnes and Noble, your blog—wherever you can.

Love, Michele

Visit www.michelezurloauthor.com for information about my other titles.

Michele Zurlo

I'm Michele Zurlo, author of the Doms of the FBI and the SAFE Security series and many other stories. I write contemporary and paranormal, BDSM and mainstream—whatever it takes to give my characters the happy endings they deserve.

I'm not half as interesting as my characters. My childhood dreams tended to stretch no further than the next book in my to-be-read pile, and I aspired to be a librarian so I could read all day. I ended up teaching middle school, so that fulfilled part of my dream. Some words of wisdom from an inspiring lady had me tapping out stories on my first laptop, so in the evenings, romantic tales flow from my fingertips.

I'm pretty impulsive when it comes to big decisions, especially when it's something I've never done before. Writing is just one in a long line of impulsive decisions that turned out to showcase my great instincts. Find out more at www.michelezurloauthor.com or @MZurloAuthor.

Lost Goddess Publishing

The Doms of the FBI Series

The SAFE Security Series

Paranormal

Anthologies

Discovering Desires Anthology by Michele Zurlo

Sneak Peek of Forging Love (unedited)

Back inside the bedroom, I found Jesse holding up a pink, battery-powered phallus. His brows knit together, and he looked very confused.

"It's a vibrator," I supplied.

He jumped, glanced at me guiltily, and almost dropped it.

Never in my life did I think I'd be able to take Jesse Foraker, the man who was unfazed by having a live grenade lobbed at his head, by surprise. I burst out laughing.

"I know what it is," he mumbled. "Where do you want it?"

"Oh, Jesse." Now that I'd done the impossible, I had to see how far I could push it. I rested my hands on his chest and leaned closer, batting my eyelashes in an exaggerated display of flirting. "Where does every woman want it?" For even greater effect, I lifted one foot behind me, though I'm not sure he would have noticed if I hadn't lost my balance.

He caught me in his strong, capable arms and set me back upright, all without actually looking at me. "You don't have a bedside table. Underwear drawer?"

I took it from him, noting that the tips of his ears were pink. "Too much? Have I made you uncomfortable?"

"No, it's—" He cleared his throat. "Fine. I, uh, I didn't think you were, you know—cleared—for that kind of thing."

I rolled my eyes like a boss. "Oh, please." Irony dripped from my tone. "That's the only part of me that didn't get broken." I had proof too—I came out of a three-year coma to find two heartbreakingly handsome, hunky men watching over me. My lips were dry and my throat hurt because of the feeding tube, but one look at Jesse, and my pussy woke right up.

I scooted the box out of the way and slipped the vibrator under my pillow. "I like to keep him nearby."

Jesse's feet shuffled, a motion I caught in my peripheral vision as I shifted my attention from the hiding spot to the box where I hoped to find towels. He wasn't a fidgety guy, so I knew he'd lied to me about being comfortable with the situation.

Never one to run away from an awkward situation, I turned to face him. Before I could get a word out, he bent his head down, and his lips grazed mine. I'd be lying if I said I didn't fantasize about this on a regular basis. All the handsomeness and other stuff aside, Jesse was a badass. An air of danger rolled from him, a vital part of his essence that made women swoon. He was equal parts scary and attractive, but I'd never been afraid of him. With me, he'd always been gentle and kind. I remembered how he'd cradled me in his arms after he'd rescued me from Cuyler. He'd watched over and sheltered me as if I was something precious and valuable.

Nobody had ever made me feel precious and valuable before. I knew it had to do with the emotion of the situation—I'd truly thought I was going to die—than with anything real.

By the time I got over the shock of being kissed for the first time in years, Jesse had one hand on the small of my back and the other in my hair cupping the back of my head. His tongue slipped into my mouth as he deepened the kiss. Shivers and tingles shot randomly through my torso as if my nerve endings had forgotten what to do with that kind of stimulation, and they thought they'd randomly fire to figure it out again.

www.ingramcontent.com/pod-product-compliance
Lightning Source LLC
Chambersburg PA
CBHW051240170626
46809CB00004B/1416